I0642192

Henry Cuyler Bunner

The runaway Browns

A story of small stories

Henry Cuyler Bunner

The runaway Browns
A story of small stories

ISBN/EAN: 9783337141264

Printed in Europe, USA, Canada, Australia, Japan

Cover: Foto ©Andreas Hilbeck / pixelio.de

More available books at **www.hansebooks.com**

THE RUNAWAY BROWNS

ADÈLE.

THE RUNAWAY BROWNS

A Story of Small Stories

BY

H·C·BUNNER

author of
"Airs from Arcady" "The Midge"
"Short Sixes" etc.

Illustrated by
C·J·TAYLOR

New York
Keppler & Schwarzmann
1892

PUCK PRESS

TO

A. L. B.

(Because You Can't Begin a Story in Philadelphia.)

T seems quite natural that the houses in Philadelphia should grow backward; yet a real Philadelphia house is always a surprise to the stranger. From the sidewalk you see what looks like a compressed mausoleum. You enter, wondering if there is going to be room for you and the one tier of defunct. Behold! that house spreads out into the silent hollow of the "square;" back-extension after back-extension, in holy privacy, in a dim and chastened respectability, you see a Philadelphia HOME expand itself.

For many, many years there came forth daily from the door of such a house as this, a gentleman who was at first Oldish, then Old, then Very Old, indeed. He was thin and tall; he wore his old-fashioned beaver hat on one side of his gaunt, old-fashioned head; his clothes had been dandified once, when dandies wore stocks and tied their collars behind. He wore them still so jauntily as to make you think you were wrong in your reckoning — if the disloyal clothes had n't gone threadbare and shiny.

A fragile, faded, prettyish, middle-aged wife said good-by to the Oldish man at the white door-step as he went forth, leaning on the arm of a thin, serious-looking young man; a fragile, fading, pretty young wife bade the Old man good-by at the same door-step as he went forth on the arm of the same young man, not quite so young now. When he was a Very Old man, neither wife bade him good-by, but a little yellow-haired boy walked on the other side of the Very Old man, while his right arm was supported by the young man, who was only young now by comparison.

He always walked as jauntily as each new year would let him, down the sunny side of Chestnut Street. All the old merchants knew him; all the solid, comfortable - looking old Friends nodded to him in a half-pitying, half- admiring way. If you asked one of them who he was, you would get this answer:

"Col. Brown, sir; Col. Orlando Brown—remarkable man, sir — great inventor — greatest mining expert in the country—made half a dozen fortunes—not worth a soumarkee — not worth a soumarkee, sir —too wild, sir—fanciful—excitable." Here the Philadelphia merchant would tap his head. "New

York man originally." And *here* the Philadelphia merchant would shake his head.

But the Colonel cared neither for their admiration or their pity; he set his hat further on one side, pulled his stock up over his collar, then pulled his collar up over his stock, ran his hand through his fine whiskers, and swaggered on his way to look at the mining-stock-list.

In New York, the Colonel would have been neither quite so much of a wonder, nor quite so much of an impracticable. He was only one of the many geniuses with whom the times can not readily keep abreast. ' He would spend years in devising new systems of milling and smelting ores — splendid systems — only, as they were about ten years ahead of the needs of civilization, civilization could make no use of them. Consequently, the Colonel had to be "temporarily accommodated" until civilization caught up with him. When she did, the Colonel drew his pay, and promptly sunk it in getting up new and still more advanced systems which the world could not possibly use for a decade at least. Meanwhile the Colonel's collars got frayed and his wives wore out.

He was like a swimmer who dives for the great seventh billow just as the fourth or fifth is rising, and comes up where he should have gone down. Thus he succeeded in keeping out of tune with the resistless surf of progress.

The Colonel died at last in the trough of the sea. When he died, he owned nothing but the roof that sheltered him and the patents that had ruined and should have enriched him.

Paul was the name of the curly-headed boy. Ernest was the name of the thin young man who had grown old holding up his father's arms. All his days, from the day he left the University of Pennsylvania to the day he left this world, his prime function in life was that of a calculating machine for the Brown patents.

It was he who had figured into practical usefulness the creations of his father's mechanical genius, balancing economies of power and speed and efficiency, one against the other. Outside of this he lived solely for hygienic reasons.

The Colonel was dead; but the patents were alive.

Ernest rented the most of the old house to a boarding-house keeper, and went to live with Paul in the last of the back-extensions, where they had a gloomy workshop on the first floor. Three times a day they issued therefrom to take their meals at the boarding-house table, where scrapple set the key of greasiness at breakfast, well sustained at dinner, and ending in a delicate diminuendo with the doughnuts at supper.

They had also retained the little stable at the rear, and here they kept two saddle-horses which it was Paul's duty to care for, and on which they took, morning and evening, a silent, sanitary ride—for the air made Ernest cough. They had no friends and they went nowhere, save that they took tea every Sunday evening at their Aunt Chambray's, an elderly lady of Huguenot extraction, who kept a rapidly decaying boarding and day school for young ladies, that had once been fashionable. It was a solemn function, held in the second story front drawing-room. When anybody opened a door downstairs, a draught came up bearing a smell—or smells —from the school-room downstairs—a smell of ink, a smell of slates, a smell of luncheon boxes and the chicken-coopy flavor of small children that you can not get out of a school-room. There were thin bread-and-butter and macaroons and tea. There was Aunt Chambray, there were Cousins Zénobie, Zaïre and Palmyre, thin, elegant, aristocratic and Roman-nosed; there was also a little third or fourth cousin, Adèle, who taught for her board, and who led a sad sort of life in the Chambray household, perhaps because she was plump and pretty and sweet-voiced, and because the way she went on with Paul was simply scandalous.

———

This was Paul Brown's life. Through their long working hours Ernest taught him all he had learned at college, and the whole science, and mystery of the Brown patents. Paul sometimes looked from his bed-room window and wondered if the stars in their courses went about with tables of logarithms in their hands.

But the day came when the calculations of Ernest Brown, of infallible Science and of irresistible Nature, all worked themselves out together. Three things happened:

First, the great Brown process was perfected, just as a vast new market rose clamoring for it. The Brown boys sold out to a New York syndicate and were rich.

Second, Ernest, having put his whole constitution into the Brown patents, lay down and calmly and placidly died.

Third, before his death he said to Paul, who was sitting by his bedside:

"Really, Paul, it is of extremely little consequence. Of course I am dying just as I have the means to indulge my tastes. But, do you know, it has lately occurred to me, on reflection, that I *have* no tastes. I think I have been in error in not cultivating some. Have *you* any tastes, Paul?"

Paul thought for a little while, then he said:
"I think I have a taste for Adèle."

The dying man looked mildly surprised. He pondered for a while.

"I think I should cultivate it," he said.

Then he turned his face to the wall.

In the Spring, Paul married Adèle.

CHAPTER I.

THEIR honey-moon was a distinct failure. What could you expect of two young people who had hardly stirred, their lives long, out of two dull, dismal old Philadelphia houses, looking out on a crossing of alleyways for their world? They went, poor lambs, in their simple ignorance, to Long Branch, where the Hebrew hosts frightened them; to Niagara Falls, where they ran into an excursion of a Western Editorial Association; and to Saratoga, where they felt as if even Divine Providence had forgotten them. They had not the first idea of traveling; they missed connections; they scattered their baggage all along their line; they got the wrong tickets; and, being the most fully developed specimen of bridal couple that had appeared for some years, they afforded unbounded amusement and great pecuniary profit to countless train-hands, porters, waiters, bell-boys, chamber-maids and hack-drivers, for the space of two weeks. Then they reached New York, went to the Fifth Avenue Hotel, and lay awake all night long wondering when the rest of the town was going to bed. In the morning Paul said:

"I am going down to see Mr. Grinridge."

"Oh, do!" said Adèle; "and *do* tell how *much* I'll thank him if he'll *only* tell us *what* to do and *where* to go! I really can't stand this another week longer. If we don't settle down *somewhere* — I'd — I'd rather go back to Philadelphia. And you know we said we'd *never* do that."

"No," said Paul, resolutely; "we won't go back to Philadelphia!" And he buttoned his coat up tight, kissed his little wife as she lay in the big hotel bed, nursing a nervous headache, and strode off to find Mr. Grinridge.

Mr. Grinridge had been the Syndicate's lawyer, and was now Paul's. He had conducted the negotiations with Ernest and Paul, and had once or twice taken Paul to lunch at the Savarin. And Mr. Grinridge was the only man in the great big world whom this poor child of a Philadelphia back-extension could call so much as an acquaintance.

Mr. Grinridge was a large, rosy, handsome, well-fed old gentleman, with beautiful curly gray hair and bright boyish eyes.

"Ah! I see," he said. "You have no friends in Philadelphia and you *have* relatives. No wonder you don't want to go back. H'm, let's see; how would New York suit you to live in?"

"Isn't it rather — noisy?" inquired Paul, dubiously.

"Oh, it strikes you so at first," said Mr. Grinridge; "but you soon get used to that. Besides, you know, you can get a quiet little flat."

Paul brightened up. He said he thought that sounded nice. So Mr. Grinridge sent a clerk with him to half a dozen agencies, where he amassed various slips of paper torn from stub-books. When he had quite a handful of these, he went back to Adèle.

Three days later a yellow-haired young man, with a haggard face and a dazed look in his eyes, walked into Mr. Grinridge's office.

"Well, have you found your flat?" said Mr. Grinridge.

"I 've found about all the flats in creation," said Paul Brown. "One more flat will drive me crazy!"

"Why, what 's the matter?" asked Mr. Grinridge.

"Matter!" said Paul; "why, it 's a nightmare. We 've seen about half the flats in New York. We 've done nothing but go up and down elevators and flights of stairs. We 've seen every kind of a flat, I believe, that ever was invented. We 've seen flats with kitchens in the front, and flats where you sleep in the dining-room and eat in the bed-rooms. We 've seen flats that you could n't turn round in, and flats as big as all outdoors. And the more we 've seen of the whole flat business, the more certain we are that we don't want to have anything to do with it. We 'd rather go and live in a cage with the animals up in Central Park."

Mr. Grinridge laughed with twinkling eyes.

"I see, I see," he said; "you are not quite up to New York pitch yet. Well, what do you say to a nice little suburban cottage? There are plenty of places convenient to the city on

Long Island, up the Hudson and over in Jersey.
You can come in and go to the theatre when you
want to, or you can stay at home and be quite
quiet and Philadelphian. Why, now that I've
grown old, I've come to that sort of thing myself.
I've settled down in just such a little hole in
the ground. Now, there's Pelham and Mt.
Vernon and Yonkers and Hastings and Morris-
town and Englewood and Plainfield — what's
the matter with one of those places?"

"What's the matter with the place where
you are?" demanded Paul.

Mr. Grinridge laughed again.

"Nothing that I know of," said he. "If you
and Mrs. Brown will lunch with me to-morrow,
we'll run out early and take a look at it. I
know of one house that ought to suit you."

They did lunch with Mr. Grinridge the next
day. It was a delightful little luncheon, and Mr.
Grinridge was so charmed with young Mrs.
Brown that he could hardly tear himself away
from the table in time to catch the early train.
But they did catch it; and very soon they were
rolling through that great broad sea of marsh
which the Jersey folk call the "medders." Then
they came to a land of low, rolling hills and un-
dulating green fields, with patches of woodland
here and there, and the whole landscape peppered
with little houses, many of them very bright and
new-looking. Little towns were strung all along
the railroad like beads on a string, and they had
come to one of the prettiest of these, which
peeped out of a nest of young green trees, when
Mr. Grinridge said: "Here we are."

Mr. Grinridge's surrey was waiting at the

station. It whirled them through a cluster of
comfortable, old-fashioned houses with first stories
of whitewashed stone; and then up into the new
part of the town, where the houses were of wood,
and quite clearly new — although they all tried
very hard to look a great deal more antique than
the real old ones. Suddenly they turned into a
broad, cheerful street with great trees along the
edge of the roadway, and with a row of low,
spreading, sloping-roofed cottages on each side.
Every house stood in a broad, generous patch of
lawn or garden. At the further end of the street

stood an old white church with a great pillared
portico in front.

"Oh!" cried Adèle, in a tone that settled it.

"Rather nice, is n't it?" said Mr. Grinridge;
"that 's my house up next to the church, and
here 's yours down here — that is, if you like it."

The June roses were blooming in the front

yard, the gravel walks were as neat as a new pin. Ampelopsis climbed over half the house, and there were scarlet-runners on the sunny side. Of course they liked it.

"It was built for the owner," said Mr. Grinridge, "but he has never occupied it. I believe he's decided to settle in California. So nobody's ever lived in the house except the caretaker, although it's been built three years. By the way, she's a very excellent and capable old woman. She put out all those flowers and things. The place was as bare as the back of my hand when she took hold of it. I should think she might be able to 'do' for you till you got settled. Her name is Mrs. Wimple."

Chapter II.

THE house was as delightful inside as out. Mrs. Wimple was a cheery, motherly old soul who could do everything that any mortal woman ever did, and who asked for no greater joy than to take a stray young married couple — or, for the matter of that, a dozen stray young married couples — under her protecting wings and " do " for them with maternal solicitude; the terms and everything else were satisfactory, and so there was nothing for the two young Browns to do but to furnish their new home and go to housekeeping.

Now this is, or ought to be, the most delightful of occupations for a young married couple. I have always been sorry for Adam and Eve that, in their first happy innocence, they started life in a ready furnished establishment. I suppose they had some fun naming the animals; but it was a poor substitute for the happiness of buying your own furniture.

But I am sorry to say the two young Browns did not enjoy this happiness any more than our first parents did, for a similar reason — they did not know enough. Home is an acquired taste. If you once acquire it, you will never want to do

without it. But if you never have acquired it —
if you have never known what it is to have a
Home — why, then, the furnishing forth of your
new house means no more to you than the obli-
gatory purchase of so many tables and chairs, and
pots and pans; and you put no more sentiment
into it than you do into buying a ton of hard coal
or a pair of suspenders — and you lose one of the
sweetest delights of human life.

That was the case of the young Browns.

It was tables and chairs to them, pots and

pans; nothing more, nothing less. They bought
a lot of very pretty things, and they put them
around the house in perfectly proper places; but
it never once occurred to them that there was any
fun in it. Mrs. Wimple enjoyed it. She shoved
the new furniture all about, and tried each thing
in a dozen different spots; but no matter where
she put it, the Browns were equally satisfied. They
always said it would "do;" and, after awhile,
Mrs. Wimple gave it up as a bad job. She *could
n't* get these young people interested in their home;
and so she went off to her kitchen and did such
wonders in the way of cookery that day after day

slipped by and they never thought of going into
the city and getting a stock of servants to supplant
her. Why should they? Mrs. Wimple, all by herself, could have supplanted any stock of servants
that was ever got together.

And yet, in spite of Mrs. Wimple and their
lesser advantages, such as health and wealth, and
youth and love, and a pretty house and pretty
things about them, and days of perfect Summer
weather in that sweet and gracious hillside country, something of the dull disappointment of their
honey-moon lingered about the life of these new-
wed Browns.

For one thing, they were lonely — though
they did n't know it. Strange as it may seem,
their neighbors in the pretty little town followed
a curious suburban fashion, and fled, at the ap-
proach of Summer, to noisy, crowded, comfortless
hotels in what they called the "real country"—
which is really the Country of Canned Vegetables. When the flowers in their gardens had given
over blooming, they would come back; but just at
present they were scattered over the face of the
earth. And so nobody came to call on the new
residents. Even Mr. Grinridge spent most of his
time at Manhattan Beach.

But it was more than mere loneliness that
troubled them. They had n't the first idea, either
of them, what to do with their lives. Paul began
to understand, vaguely, what Ernest had meant by
speaking of the necessity of cultivating tastes. He
certainly was better off than Ernest had been, in
that he had a taste for Adèle; but that taste appeared to be cultivated to its fullest extent, and
still he seemed to have a good deal of time on

his hands. And Adèle was in exactly the same plight. She loved Paul with her whole heart; but, as time passed on, she became more and more conscious of some facts that she had often taught the children at Madame Chambray's, without thinking much of their significance, namely — that there were sixty minutes in an hour and twenty-four hours in a day.

At last they got to talking frankly about it. They made up their minds that they needed occupation; but what occupation? Traveling? No; they were quite agreed that they never wanted to see a hotel again. Gardening? Botanizing? Music? Painting? Improvement of the Mind? They could n't find that they had the faintest glimmer of taste for any one of these things. Finally they hit upon Reading — and the idea came to them with all the force of an original discovery.

Now, you must remember that these two young people had been brought up in the gloomy hollows of two highly respectable Philadelphia "squares"; that their young lives had been all work and no play, and that they knew about as much of books as they did of balloons. Of course, Adèle had read such fiction as Aunt Chambray had thought suitable for a young lady in her position, which was mostly of a religious but depressing cast; and Ernest, in the exercise of his educational duties, had put Paul through Shakspere, Scott, Dickens and Thackeray, just as he had put him through Euclid and Algebra. But, as he had selected Paul's eleventh year for this course in English literature, Paul may be said to have bolted his literary diet without absorbing much of its vital essence. As to a modern novel, neither of them knew what it was. So, when they thought about it, it became quite clear to their minds that they ought to get their literature up to date.

They did it, and the way they did it was this: Paul went to New York, to the book-stand in the ferry-house, and bought all the latest novels, on the recommendation of the newsdealer. They were mostly in blue and yellow paper covers, and cost from twenty-five to seventy-five cents a-piece, though several of them had board covers and cost a dollar. Paul bought something like seven dozen of these gems of literature, and the book-stand man looked dazed for the rest of the day.

Later on, it was Paul and Adèle who looked dazed. They spent their unoccupied time — which is to say, all the time when they were not eating or sleeping — in reading those books. Paul read them aloud and Adèle listened. The books lasted two weeks. They were two weeks of murder, suicide, assassination, burglary, arson, tiger-killing, lion-hunting, elephant-shooting, car-nage, bloodshed, torture, embezzlement, heroism, sacrifice, agony, devotion, death, disease, mutila-tion, misery, vice, crime, love, glory, and every-thing else that goes to spice twenty-five-cent literature.

"My Gracious!" said Adèle, when the last book, a bright pink one, had reeled to a gory close. "And we thought life was stupid!"

Of course they did n't believe it all; for it was too good to be true. But then, if you only

believed the smallest part of it, what a world of
sport and adventure, of fire and life it was, to
charm these two children of Philadelphian respectability! And there certainly was some basis
for it all.

In a spirit of scientific inquiry, Paul got
hold of some New York papers — he had never
read anything but Philadelphia journals before —
and he caught a glimpse of life's liveliness that
fairly astonished him.

"Why," he said to Adèle, "the simple fact
is, it 's all there; but we are not in it."

How to get in it? That was the question.
Here, just outside their very gate, was a great
world of action and event going on its entertain-
ing way, while their life was as humdrum as an
unbroken routine could make it. To-day, Mrs.
Wimple gave them wheat-cakes for breakfast.
To-morrow she gave them oat-meal. Both were
excellent; and they had plenty of cream; but
sometimes they thought they would have liked a
little cold poison for a change.

They thought about it and they talked about
it in the drowsy Summer afternoons and in the
wakeful Summer evenings when you could n't feel
like going to sleep any more than the nameless
insects that sawed and filed and buzzed and
chirped in the dark depths of the foliage. And
by-and-by the Plan was born.

"Why?" said Paul, as he stalked up and
down the dainty little sitting-room, his hands in
his pockets and a scowl on his brow, "why does
nothing ever happen to us? Because we 're not
where anything happens. We 're not among the
kind of people things happen to. We are n't

acquainted with *anybody*, for the matter of that;
but we ·never should get to know that sort of
people, any way. Fancy, Mr. Grinridge saying,
'Allow me to introduce you to my friend, Mr.
Smith, who killed ninety-seven Zulus in one morning;' or, 'This is Mr. Jones, the celebrated duelist
and murderer.' I tell you, Adèle, we 're not in
the right society for adventure!"

"But how are we to get into it, Paul,
dear?" asked Adèle piteously.

"We 've got to go after it," said Paul.
"These people are n't coming to us. They must
find us as stupid as we find ourselves." He
picked up the morning paper. "Look here! 'A
Drummer Elopes with an Heiress,' 'A Peddler
Saves Three Children from Drowning,' 'Narrow
Escape of a Lightning-rod Agent,' 'A Stage-
Driver Kills a Robber,' 'Curious Adventure of a
Commercial Traveler,' 'A Tramp's Lucky Piece
of Pie.' There! those are the people who see
life — the people who move around in the world
and get among their fellow-men. Things happen
to *them*."

"But, Paul," objected Adèle, "we can't be drummers and stage-drivers and tramps and all that. You would n't like that sort of thing, I am sure."

"What 's the reason I can't?" cried Paul. "Why can't I be a drummer?"

"Because you can't drum," said Adèle.

"That 's it," said Paul, excitedly. "We live so much to ourselves that we don't know even our fellow-men. Why, you poor, dear child, a drummer is a commercial traveler! He drums up trade, don't you know?"

"But you have n't any trade to drum up, dear," said Adèle, dubiously.

"That 's just what 's the matter!" said Paul. "We 've got a lot of money and an·awfully respectable bringing-up, and a comfortable home and Mrs. Wimple and three meals a day, and nothing will ever happen to us till we die of dullness striking into a vital part. Now, suppose we had n't got the money, and had to go out into the world. We might not have so good a time, all the time; but we 'd have more different kinds of times than we 're ever likely to have the way we 're living now. And almost any different kind of a time would be a relief, would n't it, dear?"

"Paul," said Adèle, solemnly, laying down her embroidery pattern on which, for three weary weeks, she had tried to make herself believe she was working; "yesterday, do you know, I nearly fell down the front steps, and I thought I was going to sprain my ankle; and when I caught myself and did n't fall, I was really — Paul, it sounds wicked — but I was really almost sorry.

It would have been *such* a change, don't you
understand?"

"I do," said Paul. "Now, Adèle, you
listen to me!"

And he sat down beside her and whispered
in her ear.

❖   ✳   ✳

One week after that day, Mrs. Wimple,
coming downstairs in the morning, found on the
kitchen table, two letters, one
addressed to her and one to
Mr. Grinridge. Her letter
told her simply that her
employers had gone away
and would not return for a
year. She was to care for
the house in all respects as
if they were there. Mr.
Grinridge would furnish her
with money for her wages
and current expenses, upon
receipt of the letter addressed
to him.

She went upstairs, and made the tour of all
the rooms. Save for Mrs. Wimple, the house of
the Browns was as empty and desolate as though
it had never been the home of a happy young
married couple.

It was just six o'clock in the morning. Mrs.
Wimple heard the up-train choo-choo-ing off
into the distance.

The Browns had run away.

CHAPTER III

"AVE we forgotten anything?" asked Mrs. Brown of Mr. Brown, as they hurried, in a nervous, frightened way through the soft blue-gray mist of the Summer morning, making for the railroad station.

Paul Brown thought for a moment.

"I don't think we have forgotten a solitary thing," said he.

It would have been strange if they had. For one week they had done nothing but plan the details of their elopement. They had thought it all out, just as if it had been a novel of which they were to be the hero and heroine. For one year, one happy, free, irresponsible year, they were to drop out of their own private little world of respectability and dullness into that great outside world where things "happen" to people. For that year they had made every provision that could suggest itself to two youthful imaginations, stimulated by a diet of twenty-five and fifty-cent novels. Like the two little shy, secretive squirrels that they were, they had planned with a forethought that would have astonished people better skilled in the ways of the world. They had neglected nothing to insure absolute freedom and absolute privacy for twelve good months. They had left no clue to their destination; for their destination was to be determined by chance. They were prepared for all possible contingencies which might call for the use of money, for Paul had picked out half a dozen country banks, conveniently situated in the Middle and New England States, in each of which he had made a deposit in the name of an imaginary Mr. Parkins, to be drawn against by an imaginary son of the imaginary Mr. Parkins, an invalid traveling for his health, for whom Paul had constructed a very natural-looking signature. And if, by chance, the daily papers got hold of the mysterious disappearance of Mr. Brown, the young Philadelphia millionaire, and his wife, there would be nothing to connect that sensation with the appearance of a gentleman calling himself Mr. Parkins, at the counter of the Lonetown and Stray Corners Bank, for the purpose of drawing a draft to meet his traveling expenses.

Yes, it was all very well thought out, and nothing had been forgotten; but after they had passed through the old town, with its comfortable whitewashed houses, all asleep, except for the just-opening morning-glories, and, mounting the embankment on which the station stood, looked back at the red chimney of their own house, just topping the young trees, there was a queer little feeling at the two hearts of the Runaway Browns that they did not understand at all; but which any one who had ever had a home could have told them was the first beginning of homesickness. You see, in a certain sense, they *had* forgotten something.

But, as the six o'clock train came up, they got on it, and it went choo-choo-ing off with them, and they had no idea that what was troubling

them internally was anything more than the natural result of starting off without breakfast.

They had procured tickets for the Junction, where the main line crossed their little branch road and led off into the great wide world. They reached the Junction at seven o'clock, and took their first taste of the fare of the adventurous. In a small, dark, dirty eating-house, opposite the station, each of the Browns consumed two musty eggs, a slab of dead oatmeal and a saleratus-infected biscuit, and drank a cup of something which tasted brown and called itself coffee.

"Well, we ate it," said Paul, when they came out.

"Yes, dear," said Adèle; "and it seems to me that we ate a good deal of smell, too."

They bought no tickets at the Junction. They had decided to take the first train going north, and to pay their fare to the first station at which it would stop outside of the state. But the first train north did not seem to be in a hurry to come along; and so they walked up and down the platform and looked at the other people.

"Paul," said Adèle, suddenly, in a hurried whisper, "I think we 've found them."

"Found whom, dear?" inquired her startled husband.

"The people things happen to," whispered Adèle.

She pointed to a group of nine persons hud-

dled together at the extreme end of the platform. They certainly did look, not only like people to whom things might happen, in general, but like people to whom something in particular had very recently happened — something in the nature of a moral earthquake, for instance. They all wore expressions of discontent and perplexity, except one, a tall, lank, active man with an enormous black moustache, who seemed to be talking to the other eight in an encouraging, hopeful, vehement sort of way which produced absolutely no impression upon any one of them. The tall man was the sort of man that one would naturally take — or avoid —

for a particularly pushing specimen of lightning-
rod agent or tree-peddler; but the personal appearance of his companions puzzled the Browns
as much as it interested them. There were four
ladies and four gentlemen. The gentlemen were
all clean-shaven — so clean shaven that their four
chins were positively blue. They were a fat
middle-aged man, a slim young man, a man who
looked as if he might be thirty, and a long gaunt
man with an extremely prominent nose, set slightly
askew in a face that was curiously crooked, and
yet curiously agreeable. No human being could
have guessed this last man's age within ten years.
Of the ladies, one was stout and mature; of the
other three, two were comparatively and one positively young, and all decidedly good-looking. In
fact, the youngest one, who wore her curly hair
quite short, was a very pretty girl.

The clothes of these eight people were calculated to attract attention. They were both light
and loud. In the matter of trousers the men were
particularly unconventional, and the hats of the
ladies astonished Adèle. But even had they worn
the quietest of clothes, there was something about
those people that, in a strange indescribable way,
set them apart from their fellow-creatures. It was
not only the men's blue chins; it was not that the
hair of all the four ladies had a singularly unlife-
like appearance, like the tow wigs that dolls wear;
nor was it even that they all had an odd dryness
and dullness of complexion that made one think
of wax fruit in certain stages of deterioration — it
was not one of these things, it was not all of them;
but it was something which seemed to express
itself in their whole bearing and carriage, as if a

curious sort of self-consciousness was coming out
like a rash all over them.

"Did you ever see real actors off the stage?"
asked Adèle, under her breath.

"No," said Paul; "but I should think those
people must be actors. If they are n't, what else
can they be?"

"We might walk up and down the platform," said Adèle, slipping her hand into Paul's
arm.

They both of them felt a funny little thrill of
half-guilty, half-delightful excitement. It was simply human nature. There is no human being born
without the longing to "get behind the scenes":
to see the actor in his daily life: to know the real
side of that queer world of unreality. Those who
have been there are generally very willing to
testify that the people who sit in front of the
curtain get the most for their money, but nobody
ever believes them.

Paul and Adèle walked to the end of the
platform. There they found that the interesting
strangers were standing in front of the open door
of the express office. Just outside the door was a
pile of trunks of unfamiliar design, several of which
were marked in large letters: "Runyon's Dramatic
Aggregation."

Adèle pressed Paul's arm.

"They *are*," she said.

The man with the big moustache was still
talking energetically.

"I tell you, ladies and gentlemen," he said,
"it 's all right. You know me, don't you?"

"Runyon," said the tall man with the crooked
nose, who seemed to speak for the rest of the

party, "we know you too blooming well. That's what's the matter."

· The man with the crooked nose was undoubtedly an Englishman. He had a high sing-song voice that was as odd as his face.

"Well, then," said Mr. Runyon, grasping him by the lapel of his coat, with eager friendliness, "if you know me, you know I've got out of worse holes than this."

"May be you 'ave, Runyon," said the man with the crooked nose; "may be you 'ave not. We cast no aspersions on your managerial skill. But on this occasion, dear boy, you 'ave our ultipomatum. Breakfeast, dear boy, breakfast! Or I 'ock my fiddle, and back goes the Aggregation to the metropolis."

"Now, look here, Slingsby," pleaded Mr. Runyon, earnestly, "be a rational man and control

your stummick until we get to Tunkawanna. As soon as I get hold of these confounded trunks, we'll start; and when we get to Tunkawanna, I'll blow you all off to the finest breakfast you ever had in your lives. See?"

Mr. Slingsby lifted from the platform a well-worn violin case, and, opening it, he drew forth the instrument.

"This has taken me 'ome before this," he said. "It takes this Aggregation 'ome now, unless you produce for the breakfast."

The Browns were walking back to the other end of the platform.

"Paul," said Adèle, in a shocked voice, "those people ought to have their breakfast. Think how *we* felt; and we only had to wait an hour."

"Yes, my dear," said Paul; "but I can't go and offer them breakfast, you know. It might wound their pride."

"No, dear," said Adèle; "but could n't you go and offer to lend something to the — the man who has them in charge? I 'm sure he 's in a shocking position. Perhaps he 's lost his pocket-book."

"Well," said Paul, rather dubiously, "I might go and see what 's the matter."

"Go now," said Adèle, quickly. "See, he 's left the others. I 'm sure he 's going to do something desperate."

Paul hurried off to Mr. Runyon, and caught him just as he was leaving the platform. A minute after that, Adèle noticed that Mr. Runyon had Paul by the lapel of his coat and was talking to him as earnestly as he had been talking to Mr. Slingsby. After a few minutes, Paul came back to Adèle. His manner betrayed some excitement.

"It 's a most outrageous case of persecution," said Paul. "This man Runyon has in-

vested all the savings of his lifetime in taking this company out on a tour of the provinces."

"The provinces?" said Adèle. "What are the provinces?"

"Well," said Paul, doubtfully, "so far, they seem to be New Jersey. Anyway, that 's what he said. And he paid a man in New York ten thousand dollars for a play — it 's called 'A Perfect Pet' — and he had a partner who was going to put up half the money, and the partner 's run away and left him in the lurch; and now he 's got so far on his trip, and some brute of a hotel-keeper is suing him for some debts that his partner contracted when he was here once before; and the man 's got a judgement on his trunks for $37.15. And they had nothing but paper in the house last night."

"What does that mean?" asked Adèle.

"I don't know," said Paul; "but it must be something in the nature of notes. He did n't get any cash, anyway. And now he says the play is on the very verge of a great success, and they 're certain to make a lot of money at Tunkawanna to-night, if he can only get his trunks and get there. He says that of course he could stay here and fight the lawsuit, and he can get plenty of money from New York, but that will take time; and if he misses his engagement to-night, his whole tour will be ruined and he 'll lose all the money he has invested. I think he said he put $39,000 into the play."

"Dear me!" said Adèle; "it 's the meanest thing I ever heard of! Could n't you go to the hotel-keeper and explain it to him?"

"I am afraid that would n't do much good," said Paul; "but I could lend Mr. Runyon the money he needs to pay the judgement. I proposed that to him; of course it was a very delicate matter — but he was very nice about it. He 'll give me his note, of course. And then —"

"Well?" queried Adèle.

"Why, he says," continued Paul, "that it 's a splendid opening for a partner."

"For a partner?" queried Adèle, in amazement.

"Yes," said Paul, with heightened color; "for a partner."

"But, Paul, dear," said Adèle, dubiously, "is n't it just like that other business you wanted to go into — fifing? drumming? — What did you call it? How can you be an actor's partner, if you are n't an actor yourself?"

"But, my dear," said Paul, "he 's not an actor, he 's a manager; don't you see?"

"Yes," said Adèle, "but you are n't. How can you be partners with a manager?"

"Why," said Paul, "don't you understand? It 's just like my business with the syndicate. I know all about my patents, and I put up that

knowledge against their capital. Now this is a
precisely similar case. This man knows all about
the business of managing, and he puts up that
against my capital. He 's been thirty years in the
business. Now he puts up all that experience
against my capital."

"But do you think that 's quite fair to the
man, Paul?" asked Adèle, looking a little wor-
ried, "if he puts up all those thirty years' experience and you put up only $37.15?"

"Oh, well," said Paul, with some embarrass-
ment, "it will be a little more than that. He says
they 'll probably need a little ready money to
start with. And then, you know, we need n't
consider it from a business point of view. And,
of course, we can dissolve partnership whenever
we 're tired of traveling with them."

Adèle opened her eyes wide.

"Oh, are we going to travel with them?"

"Why, of course, that 's the idea," said Paul.

"What, with all those — ladies?" asked
Adèle.

"Why," said Paul, "don't you like them?"

"Oh, ye-es," said Adèle, in a doubtful tone.

She looked hard at the four ladies for a moment. Then her face brightened.

"I suppose, Paul," she said, "that if they make a great deal of money at Tunk — what 's its name? — they 'll buy this year's hats?"

"Why, yes; I suppose so," said Paul. "Are n't those this year's hats?"

"No, dear," replied Adèle, very decidedly, "they 're not — not the least little bit in the world. And I 'm sure," she added reflectively, "I don't know what year's hats they *are*."

"Well, dear, what do you say?" demanded Paul.

Adèle reflected for a moment.

"We wanted to have something happen," she said. "Well, Paul, I think we 've got our chance."

CHAPTER IV.

WHEN the train rolled into Tunkawanna
that afternoon at five o'clock, the
Browns felt as if their new friends
were very old friends indeed. Nine
friendlier people they had never met
— excepting Mr. Runyon, who traveled
all the way in the baggage car; and, though
he did not state his reason for this somewhat
peculiar proceeding, he left them in such a frank,
simple, unaffected manner that they saw clearly
that he did not wish to keep them on formal
terms.

As for the members of the company, it did
not require more than ten minutes to establish an
acquaintance with them. Mr. Slingsby not only
introduced them all, but in a private chat with
the Browns supplied various scraps of interesting
information. "They are n't a nasty crowd to
travel with," he said. "In my time, my boy, I 've
traveled with many a nastier. Delancey—that 's
that good-looking, pleasant, blue-eyed jackass in
the third seat down on the other side of the car
— he 's playing our lead. He can't act—but
then, my boy, how many leading men *can* act?
That fat man with him is named Weegan. He
comes from Peoria, and he thinks he 's a low
comedian. At 'ome—in England, you know—

when I was a youngster, they used such people
for clowns in pantomimes. But we 've got to take
the world as we find it."

"Which do you mean?" inquired Paul; "the
fat man with the diamond pin in his neck-tie?"

"Great Heavens, sir!" cried Mr. Slingsby, in
a tone of withering contempt; "*that* man?" And
he pointed to the stouter of the two stout men,
who was placidly nodding off to sleep. "Is it
possible — is it possible that you don't know
Mingies?"

"I — I —" stammered Paul.

"No, my boy," said Mr. Slingsby, in a re-
signed singsong; "you don't know Mingies, and
you don't know *Me*. But if it was n't for Mingies, sir, I would n't be in this blooming barn-
storming company. No, sir; my self-respect
would n't permit it. There are just two actors in
this company, my boy, and Mingies is the other
one." Here Mr. Slingsby observed a troubled
look on Paul's face, and hastened to add: "Understand me, my dear boy, it 's an elegant company for the road. I am talking simply from
an artistic standpoint. Now the *ladies*," he went
on hurriedly, "the ladies are uncommonly strong.
There are Miss La Tourette and Miss Obrian just
in front of us," he whispered. "Young things;
and they can't act much, — but who does act
much nowadays, my boy? That lady with the
short hair is Miss Georgie Mingies. She has n't
her father's talent, but she 's a fine girl — a fine
girl, sir."

"And who," asked Adèle timidly, "is the
elderly lady in the small hat?"

Mr. Slingsby started in genuine surprise.

"Bless my soul!" he exclaimed, "where did you two people come from?"

"Philadelphia," said Adèle.

"Ah!" said Mr. Slingsby. "That lady is Mrs. Sophia Wilks, formerly of Covent Garden, London. Everybody on this broad continent, except yourselves, my children, knows her as Aunt Sophy. When I first knew that lady, sir, she was one of the most charming soubrettes in the profession, and the most beautiful woman on the English stage. That was thirty years ago, my boy. Have you a cigar about you?"

Mr. Slingsby got a cigar and went into the smoking-car to smoke it. Then Mrs. Wilks lurched across the aisle and sat down in the seat opposite the Browns.

"My dears," she said affably, "don't believe

one word that that man Slingsby tells you. He's a very nice fellow, but he'll never be an actor if he lives to be as old as Methusalem. I don't say he can't play the violin; but as for acting, why, bless your souls, it ain't in the man."

"I don't understand it," said Paul to Adèle,

in a moment when they happened to be left alone; "it seems none of them can act except Mr. Mingies."

"And he 's asleep," said Adèle.

It had begun to rain when they reached Tunkawanna. Perhaps this is not a very accurate way of describing what had happened to the weather; for, such a sturdy, vigorous, well-established rain must have had its beginning several states off. It poured in great heavy sheets, through which they dimly descried an uninteresting town of low, brick houses, all very dirty and dingy with the smoke from the collieries, whose tall chimneys, high up on the neighboring hills, shot up flashes of deep red flames. The town of Tunkawanna, in truth, was little more than one dull, long, mean street, straggling along the edge of the broad river, whose further shore was lost in the wet darkness, out of which came the sound of its swift rushing, clearly to be heard above the roar of the rain.

Adèle slipped her hand into Paul's arm as she gazed down the dismal street.

"Oh, Paul," she whispered; "how awfully gloomy!"

"Gloomy it is," said Mr. Slingsby, just behind them; "and not an umbrella in the 'ole crowd."

"Runyon, my dear," said Aunt Sophia cheerfully to her manager, "you are standing treat to umbrellas, I suppose, as usual?"

Adèle pressed Paul's arm, and he spoke up hastily.

"Perhaps it would n't be convenient —," he began, "I mean — if Mr. Runyon will permit me — I 'll be very happy—"

"To set up the umbrellas?" broke in Mr. Slingsby. "Ah, my boy, I knew you were a thoroughbred from the moment I laid my eyes on you. Come with me, and I 'll show you an elegant establishment."

The two gentlemen dashed through the rain across the street to a little shop where a very little Hebrew boy, whose head hardly came across the counter, opened his dark and dreamy eyes astonishingly wide at receiving an order for eleven umbrellas. Then he gasped once and recovered his self-possession.

"Make it one dozen," he said, "un' I gif you a discount."

"Take him," said Mr. Slingsby, nudging Paul; "the extra one may come in 'andy."

They returned to the station, and, leaving

Mr. Runyon to superintend the men who were to take the trunks to the theatre, the Aggregation started up the street, Aunt Sophy piloting the two Browns.

"I have played in this town eleven times," said she; "and every time it rained, except one, and then there was an earthquake."

The gentlemen of the company had dropped behind. From time to time Adèle missed the sound of their feet. This puzzled her a little, and after a while she looked over her shoulders. She observed that, although the four gentlemen had started with five umbrellas, they were now clustered under one. And even as she looked she saw them suddenly deviate from the straight path and disappear into one of the numerous liquor-saloons scattered along the way. When they came out they had no umbrella at all. But they wiped their mouths and turned up their coat-collars, and trudged cheerily along in the rain.

Thus they reached the Tunkawanna hotel, which was quite the smallest, darkest and dirtiest hostelry that Paul and Adèle had ever seen. Mr. Runyon had already passed them, seated on his truck-load of trunks, and at the door of the hotel they found him earnestly conversing with the proprietor. He had the proprietor by the lapel of his coat, and the proprietor was shaking his head in a stubborn sort of way. As soon as Mr. Runyon saw Paul, he hurriedly drew him aside.

"This is a peculiar sort of place, Mr. Brown," said he, "and they've got a sort of invariable rule about getting their pay in advance. I am an old friend of the proprietor's, but he says

he can't break it even for me. You understand?
I told him you 'd see to it as soon as you came."

"Oh, certainly," said Paul.

Paul went into the office, where he paid the
hotel proprietor $8.25. The proprietor swept it
into his till and shut the drawer with a loud slam.
As the lock snapped, he whistled a brief and
peculiar melody which Paul vaguely remembered
having heard as a boy.

"What is that tune?" he inquired of the
proprietor, for there seemed to him something
peculiarly suggestive about it.

"'Over the fence is out,'" said the proprietor.

CHAPTER V

"DEAR me, Paul!" said Adèle, "I never should know this was a theatre if it was n't for the smell."

They had eaten a curious and unpleasant meal at the Tunkawanna hotel, and now they sat in a curious and unpleasant little den at the extreme rear of the Tunkawanna Opera House. They hardly knew how they had got there. They had gone through the stage door with a little shiver of delightful expectation. Then they had shivered in another way as cold draughts had poured on them from every direction. They had felt their way through dark passages, and climbed up rickety stairs. They had rubbed against walls greasy with the touch of many hands, dusty walls, and walls coated thick with whitewash. Then, with a consciousness of being smirched and disheveled, they had emerged upon the stage of the theatre, a barn-like place where three or four men were clumsily arranging tall wooden frames covered with canvas. The canvas was splashed with great daubs of pale dull color.

"Is it really *scenery*, Paul?" asked Adèle.

"I am afraid it is," said Paul, vaguely discerning in the dull blots and splotches something that seemed like a dim caricature of trees and foliage. But, oh! how disappointing it all was! How bare, how cold, how lifeless, how dismal! All the light came from a row of gas jets on the top of what looked like an overgrown music stand, from which a long rubber pipe trailed off into the darkness. Beyond this line of light they saw a gloomy cavern with rows of empty seats, the backs of which were staring at them in an unfriendly way.

It did not seem possible that they had sat in just such seats and gazed, enraptured, on scenes of glowing color and graceful form. They both felt for the moment as if they had been cheated out of every dollar they had ever paid for going to theatres.

Then Mr. Runyon saw them, and called them up to be introduced to the proprietor of the Opera House.

He was a very fat Jewish gentleman, Mr. Jacobs, who had little attention to pay to them, being too much employed in using unkind language to the stage-hands. They caught a few glimpses of the members of the company, who had assorted themselves among various small dens at the back of the stage, from which they occasionally came forth in progressive stages of disfigurement, their faces smeared with paint and spotted with patches of impossible hair. It was all a dreary nightmare, the more ghastly that it seemed extremely business-like, and that the two lonely Browns had no place in it. It was really a relief when Mr. Runyon, remembering their existence, hustled them into a bleak little room overhanging the rushing river, which he said was the greenroom.

"You 'd better sit here a bit," he said, "and be out of the way."

They could n't help feeling that they were very much in the way.

"Paul, dear," said Adèle, "*so* far, I don't think the theatrical business is very nice, do you?"

Paul was looking out of the window over the river.

"It is n't very cheerful," he replied. "But, Good Gracious, Adèle! Look here!"

Adèle joined him at the window and peered with him into the darkness below.

"Why, Paul," she said, "it 's Mr. Slingsby. What *is* he doing?"

It *was* Mr. Slingsby. He was standing just under the window, on the stone wall that curbed the river bank, and he was carefully examining the fastening of a rowboat that was tossing restlessly on the swollen breast of the stream. After a moment or two he was joined by Mr. Mingies and a boy, who carried a trunk

between them. They exchanged a few words in a whisper, and then they lowered the trunk into the boat, and the boy rowed off into the darkness. In a few minutes he returned, but the trunk was not in the boat. Mr. Slingsby and Mr. Mingies, who had retired into the theatre building, reappeared with another trunk, and the boy rowed it away in the same manner. Three times was this mysterious performance repeated. Then Adèle, remembering the fate of the umbrellas, cried out suddenly:

"Why, Paul, they can't be exchanging those trunks for things to drink!"

Both of the gentlemen on the bank below started violently, as they heard Adèle's voice. They looked up and saw the two faces at the window and then each of them laid a finger on his lips, and said "Sh-h-h-h!" in a very significant and tragic manner.

"Mr. Slingsby," said Paul, severely, "are we deceived in you? What does this mean?"

"Sh-h-h-h!" said Mr. Slingsby again. "It 's all right, dear boy; 'pon me honor it 's all right."

"What are you doing with those trunks?" demanded Paul.

"Sh-h-h-h!" hissed Mr. Slingsby. "For 'eaven's sake, *sh-h-h-h!!* Is Runyon there?"

"No," said Paul.

"Look over your shoulder," whispered Mr. Slingsby. "'E 's a devil for snooping."

"I tell you," said Paul, "we are alone. But I want to know what you are doing with those trunks."

"Dear boy," hissed Mr. Slingsby, waving his hands wildly, "just listen to your old uncle for one minute. They 're after Runyon again!"

"Who are?" asked Paul.

"Why, the Sheriffs," said Mr. Slingsby. "They always are, you know. There are more judgements out against Runyon than any man in the country."

"And they are right onto him in Tunka-wanna," said Mr. Mingies, solemnly.

"That they are," Mr. Slingsby chimed in. "It 's good-by to the trunks if they get them here. There 's two of the Sheriff's men in front of the house now. Jacobs is trying to bluff them, but it won't be any use. There 's nothing for us to do but to get out, and get out quick. You lower your wife down out of that window, and drop after her. Let her down easy and you can just get her feet on my shoulders. I 've taken ladies out of that window before."

"But what 's going to become of the play to-night?" cried Adèle. "How can they have any play if you all run away?"

"There won't be any play to-night," said Mr. Delancey, emerging from the door beneath the Browns," unless Runyon plays the Sheriff for a sucker. And that ain't likely. We 've been here five times before."

"'Urry up," said Mr. Slingsby, beseechingly; "the ladies will be here in a minute. They are just washing up and getting their things on."

"Do you mean," said Paul, in a voice of indignation, "that we are to run away from the Sheriff?"

"You bet," said Mr. Delancey, flippantly; "and mighty lively, too."

"Well," said Paul, "I will not be a party to any such proceedings. I am Mr. Runyon's part-ner, and whatever legal difficulties he may have gotten into, I will stay and face them out with him."

Here Mr. Mingies spoke forth for the first time, in the full round voice of authority.

"Young man," he said, "you are young. From your looks I should take you to be twenty-five, and from your experience of the world I am led to think that you are about nineteen. If you remain in this town of Tunkawanna to fight the judgements that Runyon has run up in the last fifteen years, you will be a middle-aged man before you get through with the last case. Now you take the advice of one who has had experience in this profession. You have a wife there. Let her down easy out of that window, and we'll be in the State of Pennsylvania inside of fifteen minutes. Mr. Slingsby will assist the lady."

Mr. Slingsby promptly backed up to the wall, braced his tall form against it, squared his shoulders, and, with knightly courtesy, dropped his chin upon his breast. A moment later, Adèle was gently lowered to the ground by three pairs of gallant hands.

The Brown family found some difficulty in getting into the stern of the boat, for the water was high and rough, and the stone wall was slippery. Adèle clung closely to Paul. The black night frightened her, the roar of the river, and the fitful, furious onslaughts of the wind and rain.

It brought a sense of positive comfort to her heart to hear the cheerful, motherly voice of Aunt Sophy Wilks, and to see her massive form descending into the boat. Mrs. Wilks was as calm and unperturbed as though

she were the Queen of England receiving her
friends.

"Ah, my dear," she said, "it 's you, is it?
Glad you 're going to be with us. But this
sporting life is killing me. It 's too volatile and
I 'm too weighty. Say, boys," she continued,
addressing the gentlemen on the bank, "you 'd
better hurry up. I think they 've got Runyon."
Mr. Delancey put his head in the black doorway
and called softly up the stairs:

"Hi, girls," he said; "hurry up!"

A minute passed, and then the two Browns,
rocking madly in the rowboat, which the boy
vainly tried to steady with the oars, looked up
and saw four more dark figures appear upon the
wet and wind-swept stone wall.

With many little muffled cries of fright, the
ladies were lowered into the boat. There were
two pairs of oars, and Mr. Delancey took one pair.

"It 's a good thing, Delancey," said Mr
Slingsby, "that you can *row*."

He laid a peculiar and severe emphasis upon
the word "row," which must have conveyed an
unpleasant meaning to Mr. Delancey, for he
frankly and simply responded:

"You be damned."

"Cast off!" said Mr. Mingies to the boy,
with the air of a Rear Admiral.

The boy clambered up to the top of the
bank and began to struggle with the knot of the
painter, while the ten people in the rowboat
huddled together in their crowded quarters, and
tried to trim the craft.

"Aunt Sophy," inquired Mr. Slingsby, "are
you dead over the keel?"

"If I was an inch to one side," replied Aunt Sophy gravely, "it would be the end of this boat-load."

And then for a moment it seemed as if the end had come. That furious last gust which rounds up a great storm struck them as suddenly as a flash of lightning, snapping the painter as if it had been a thread, and drove the boat into the angry, rushing current of the river. The women shrieked as they were swept into the dark-

ness; and, blacker than all the black things about them, the great arches of the railroad bridge loomed up in their path. Then the torrent swept them madly through that dim gateway; and as they rushed on into the howling darkness, Mingies, who had cast one hasty look behind, remarked casually :

"Runyon got out the back window."

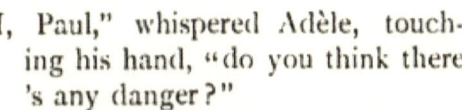

Chapter VI

H, Paul," whispered Adèle, touching his hand, "do you think there 's any danger?"

"No," said Paul, reassuringly; "not the least." But his heart sank as he put his arm around his wife and drew her close to him.

"Oh, Paul," she cried with a gasp, "how wicked we were not to be content!"

Just as she spoke, there was a sound like a pistol shot, and Mr. Delancey was thrown off his seat into the bottom of the boat. Then he scrambled up with a white face and reached out madly over the side. One of his oars had broken and the other had been torn from his hand.

Adèle hid her face on Paul's breast, and the two sat silent. But their companions were not silent. Their voices rose up in cries that ought to have been heard on either shore, and they must have rushed for ten minutes through that black and howling tempest before Slingsby and Mingies, who alone retained something like self-possession, could induce them even to sit still and minimize the risk of capsizing.

"Is that Aunt Sophy yelling like that?" shouted Mr. Slingsby from the bow to Mr. Mingies in the stern. "Don't let her move, Mingies!"

"I 'm sitting in her lap," shouted back the ponderous, but long-headed Mr. Mingies, "or we 'd have been at the bottom before this."

For some space the boat was whirled along, but whether they were hours or minutes in the power of the tempest, not one could tell. They had lost all sense of direction; they could not even see the whitecapped water ten feet from the boat, and it seemed as though they were being hurled into infinite space through eternal night.

Suddenly they stopped with a crash and a jar that threw them in all directions. The chorus of shrieks arose again as the boat went to pieces under them and let them down into the water.

They did not have very far to go, however. Paul and Adèle found themselves sitting in a great deal of mud and very little water; and as the truth broke upon the minds of the others, that they were in no immediate danger of drowning, their alarm gradually subsided.

"Take 'old of 'ands," cried the ever-ready Mr. Slingsby. "We 'll make a line and strike for the shore. Where are you, Mingies?"

The voice of Mr. Mingies boomed suddenly out of the darkness.

"Here," he said, in a tone of deep feeling. "And Mrs. Wilks and I are settling about six inches every minute."

Just here they heard a shriek that was without doubt from Aunt Sophia.

"What 's the matter there, Mingies?" Mr. Slingsby called out.

There was great relief expressed in Mr. Mingies's voice as he cheerfully bellowed back:

"It 's all right, now, Slingsby; it 's all right. Mrs. Wilks has touched rock."

After a good deal of groping in the darkness, the more active members of the party formed a line, and each holding the other firmly by the hand, they began to feel their way toward the shore, through a darkness that seemed even deeper than they had previously encountered. Suddenly they were startled by a profane remark from Mr. Slingsby, who led the line.

"What is it?" cried Mr. Delancey, apprehensively.

"I bumped my head," replied Mr. Slingsby.

"Bumped your head?" cried his friends, in amazement.

"Against what?" demanded Paul.

"Against the Washington Monument, I should say by the feel of it," answered Mr. Slingsby, in his plaintive singsong. "It 's 'arder than my 'ead, whatever it is."

"Oh, Paul," cried Adèle, desperately, "where do you suppose we are?"

"Slingsby," said Mr. Mingies, solemnly, "do you remember that when we were here, five years ago, we had a little picnic down the river?"

"Yes," said Mr. Slingsby.

"A very enjoyable occasion?" continued Mr. Mingies.

"Yes," said Mr. Slingsby.

"Under the shore arch of a stone bridge?" pursued Mr. Mingies.

"Yes," said Mr. Slingsby.

"Well," said Mr. Mingies, "we are under that arch now. I can see the lights of the tavern on the other side of the river."

"Begad, you're right," said Mr. Slingsby. "Let's have another picnic!"

"Certainly," said Mr. Mingies; "the moon is just coming out."

The storm had sunk a little, and one or two patches of light had appeared in the black sky, affording just enough illumination to reveal their situation to the castaways. It was far from pleasant. They were ashore, certainly; but the water had risen so high that it had covered everything except a little pile of rocks that lay against one side of the great arch, midway between its two ends. Mr. Slingsby painfully groped his way, first to right and then to left, and reported deep water in both directions. Mr. Delancey was with great difficulty induced to lead an exploring party down the stream, but, although he wore no watch, he refused to go in deeper than his watch-pocket, and came back in disgust. Paul tried to stem the current and to get up-stream, but after stepping into a hole and finding the water on a level with his ears, he agreed with Adèle that his duty was to stay by her side.

"There appears to be," said Mr. Slingsby, who was fumbling around and trying to familiarize

himself with the boundaries of his pile of rocks,
" a species of peninsula here which might at least
accommodate the ladies. The sterner sex can sit
at the base of the throne, as it were, and let the
water flow through their trousers."

" A great mind that Slingsby has," said Mr.
Weegan, who happened to be standing next to
Paul. " It 's a pity he can't act."

By dint of hard work the ladies were got
upon the rocks. The entire party was obliged
to form a line to haul Mr. Mingies and Mrs.
Wilks from their anchorage; but finally five wet,
cold, shivering women were pushed up the slippery stones, where they huddled together against
the masonry. Below them the men crowded as
far out of the water as they could get. And thus
they disposed themselves to await the dawn.

The river rushed madly by, roaring through
the great hollow of the arch. The wind poured
in on them in a way that made even the stout-
hearted Slingsby observe that there was more
draught than he cared about. Adèle sobbed
quietly, with her head on Paul's shoulder.

" Oh, dear! " she said, " who would have
thought it could have been so wicked just to
want a little change? Don't you feel horribly
wicked, Paul? "

" I feel wet," said Paul.

Their teeth chattered, and their bones
ached. Even Mr. Slingsby could joke no longer.
Everybody was sinking into a dull stupor of
misery, except Aunt Sophia Wilks, who was
moving around on the topmost stone of the heap,
in a way that excited the attention of Miss
Mingies.

"Aunt Sophy," she cried, "what *are* you doing?"

About this time the rest of the shipwrecked travelers became conscious of a peculiar, yet an agreeable and familiar odor, which overcame the smell of the river and the damp stones.

Mr. Mingies rose to his feet.

"Georgie," he demanded, "did you have a bottle of cologne in your pocket?"

"Yes, Papa," said Miss Mingies.

"Then Aunt Sophy's got it. Take it from her."

But here the voice of Mrs. Wilks rose in indignant protest.

"I scorn your insinuations," she cried; "and if my 'usband was not in his grave you would not dare address such language to me. Cologne, indeed!"

"Have you got it?" asked Mr. Mingies of Miss Mingies.

"Paul," demanded Adèle, in a horrified whisper, "what is cologne made of?"

"It is principally alcohol, I believe, my dear," answered Paul.

"Oh, if my 'usband were here," wailed Mrs. Wilks. "Oh, Robert, Robert!"

Mr. Mingies resumed his seat in the river. "It is the last infirmity of a noble mind," he said, "and I hope it will keep her warm."

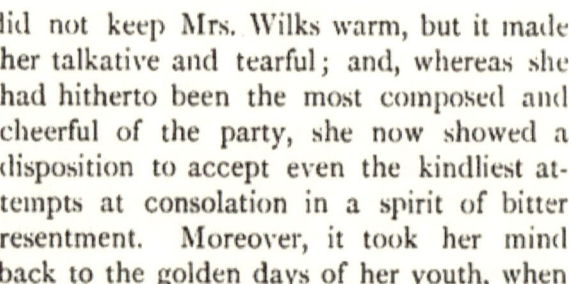

CHAPTER VII

T did not keep Mrs. Wilks warm, but it made her talkative and tearful; and, whereas she had hitherto been the most composed and cheerful of the party, she now showed a disposition to accept even the kindliest attempts at consolation in a spirit of bitter resentment. Moreover, it took her mind back to the golden days of her youth, when she had reveled in luxury and had known the protecting care of a husband.

The spell of old memories must have been strong upon Mrs. Wilks, for she occasionally dropped her "H's."

Her lamentations were fitful, being interrupted by brief stretches of slumber, from which she would wake to wail over her lot, and to call upon her departed helpmate.

"Never, never," she cried, "was I accustomed to this sort of thing, nor educated for it! Oh, if I 'ad you 'ere, my 'usband! Oh, George, George!"

"Paul," whispered Adèle in his ear, "did you hear that? She spoke of her husband as George, and I am sure she called him Robert just a little while ago."

"Yes, dear," said Paul, "and I think you must have had a little nap, or you would have heard her refer to him some time ago as Alexander."

"Oh, Paul, dear," Adèle whispered, "this is dreadful!"

"Look there!" cried Paul, suddenly; "there's the sun!"

It is only at times such as these that commonplace folk realize something of the beauty of that miracle that occurs three hundred and sixty-five times in every year — the birth of a new day. The Browns had come out for adventure, and to see what life had to show them; and in that moment they both felt that they were looking upon one of the most beautiful things that had ever happened to the earth. And yet they might have seen it any day in the year out of any one of their east windows.

"How heavenly!" whispered Adèle in hushed rapture.

"Yes," said Paul; "and that's the tavern right over there on the other side of the river."

"That's so," said Adèle, looking, with a new interest in her brown eyes, at the low, comfortable white building that began to rise above

the river mist, among a clump of huge willows
just across the stream.

"Does n't it seem to you, Paul, as if you
had never thought before just what a nice thing
breakfast is, too?"

"I 'm going to have some breakfast," said
Paul, "if I have to swim for it. Here, let 's
wake these people up. I 'm blessed if they
are n't all asleep."

"I don't believe," remarked Adèle, reflectively, "that they mind *anything*. But don't
wake them up for just a minute — look, dear!"

They were both of them stiff and sore and
tired; but, as they looked out upon the new
morning, it was all so fresh and fair, so bright
from its bath of rain, so tender in its summery
greens, softened by the delicate gray haze that
hung over the river and lifted a little and then
faded out from the face of Nature, as if to cheat
the eye, that they could think of nothing but the
beauty before them; and their awakening hearts
were stronger than their stiffened limbs.

Like the light of eyes that awake and look
into the face of a loved one, the landscape came
out of the mist. They were far away from the
town, out in the happy country. The broad river
flowed by them, still rippling in its fullness, but
clear and pure. There were green fields and
patches of woodland on either side, and right
opposite them that comfortable and home-like
looking tavern stood white among the great green
willows with their brownish-yellow trunks. And,
as they stepped out upon the stones that the
rapidly subsiding waters had left bare, they saw
the graceful line of the big stone bridge reaching

across to the other side, arch after arch, bearing
on its broad shoulders the road that led to the
open door of the old hostelry. The door was
open; they could see it from where they stood on
the stones, with the water just at the soles of their
shoes. And it seemed as if Breakfast actually
beckoned to them from that welcoming portal.

They stood there for a minute or two, and
took a brief proprietorship in the sun and the sky
and the green woods and the quick rushing river,
and then they set about wakening their companions. Mrs. Wilks was the most difficult to
rouse. For a long time she only grunted in an
amiable way, as often as Paul shook her. At last
she opened her eyes and said, as one talking in a
dream :

" Cologne? No, never. I deny it!"

And then she rubbed her eyes and awoke
definitively. A puzzled look came into her face
as she put her hand to her head.

"Where did I get it?" she inquired of Miss
Georgie Mingies.

" My cologne," said Miss Mingies, simply.

"I'll give you another bottle, my dear," said Mrs. Wilks. "Just as soon as the luck turns."

"Aunt Sophy," said Miss Mingies, with impressive decision, "you always were a lady."

"She always was," returned Mr. Slingsby, pleasantly. "Now, will the lady wade, or will she go out of this pick-a-back?"

"Are n't you broke enough as it is?" inquired Aunt Sophy, who was evidently fast recovering the use of her faculties. "I'll walk, as far as I'm concerned. I'd like to rinse off a little."

There was no longer any difficulty in getting out of their uncomfortable quarters, and the bedraggled party slowly but safely made its way to the shore, and started over the bridge toward the tavern. Each member of the group was becoming conscious of a new stiffened joint at each step of the way.

"Did you ever see a second-hand set of marionettes?" said Mr. Slingsby.

Paul had never had that experience.

"Well, that's the movement we've got on us," said Mr. Slingsby.

With the soft glow of the early morning sun illuminating their damp and clinging garments, the remains of the Aggregation and the two Browns presented themselves at the tavern-door. They were all partners in misery and equals in misfortune, so far as the eye could see. There was nothing now to distinguish Mrs. Brown's hat, in respect to social position, from even the worst of those worn by her sisters in distress, which was unquestionably the strange and towering structure that topped the head of Mrs. Wilks.

And yet they smiled as they looked at each other, and not with the derisive smile with which the inn-keeper regarded them, but with the happy and innocent smile which children at their play exchange with one another. Wet and stiff and sore, fellowshipping with vagabonds in the same plight as themselves, the Browns were having a good time.

"Well, you *are* a healthy looking lot!" said the fat, red-faced landlord, as he gazed upon them. "Be'n out in the wet, ain't you?"

"Damn his impudence!" said Mr. Slingsby to Paul. "He thinks there is n't any money in the crowd. He little knows—"

Here a sudden misgiving caused Mr. Slingsby to change his confident expression.

"Say," he whispered, anxiously, "you *have* got some scads, have n't you?"

"Scads?" repeated Paul, doubtfully.

"Yes. Plunks — gold — spondulix — cash —money, you know," exclaimed Mr. Slingsby. "Runyon did n't get away with all you had, did he?"

"No," said Paul, smiling. "I think I have enough for our present necessities."

"Oh, it's all right," said Mr. Slingsby, much relieved. "Then see me jump on that brute's neck!"

And Mr. Slingsby straightened himself up and infused into his person an air of grandeur, which not even his dampness could diminish. Then he sternly advanced upon the landlord.

"Are you intoxicated?" he demanded severely, and in so peremptory a tone that the landlord gasped rather than said:

"Naw!"

"Then," said Mr. Slingsby, "your insolence is inexcusable." He turned with a lofty air to Miss Mingies, who was trying to look unconcerned while she pinned up a gap in the rear of her skirt. "Lady Georgianna," he said, waving his hand toward Mrs. Wilks, who showed indications of being about to go to sleep standing, "will you kindly conduct the Countess into that apology for an apartment which I see on my right? And Lord Delancey will see to the comfort of the rest of the ladies, while I give my orders to this fellow. Baron," he continued, addressing Paul, "I shall need your advice in the preparation of a menu for our breakfast. I suppose this person can be taught to serve something eatable."

Then, haughtily signaling to the landlord to follow him, he strode into the barroom.

The landlord's eyes almost started from his head.

"You had better make haste," observed Mr. Delancey, with a stern, yet condescending manner. "Lord Slingsby is in no mood to be trifled with. Is it not strange," he said to Mrs. Brown, "that when one's carriage breaks down, it always breaks down where there is nothing better than such a hole as this within ten miles? But I suppose you can't expect anything better in this blarsted country."

The landlord was by this time of a fine, rich purple color. He made one or two vain attempts to speak; but finding that he only produced a sort of stifled gurgle, he gave it up, and meekly followed Mr. Slingsby into the barroom.

The landlord had a bad quarter of an hour with Mr. Slingsby in the barroom. Mr. Slingsby opened the proceedings by asking Paul, in an off-hand manner, if he remembered what he had done with the bill-of-fare from the Hôtel Aristocratique.

"That was a fairly satisfactory repast," he observed, "and may afford us some suggestions. I think you put it in your wallet, dear boy."

Twenty-four hours before, Paul would probably have asked him what he meant, or told him outright that he knew nothing of any bill-of-fare or any Hôtel Aristocratique. But now it was with a feeling of having been born into a new world, and a world where, even under the most depressing conditions, life seemed to have a wonderful lot of fun about it, that Paul impressively produced his comfortable-looking pocketbook — it was wet and out of shape, but its contents gave it a look of comfort — carelessly pulled out a ten dollar bill or two in a pretended search for the imaginary menu, and then told Mr. Slingsby that he thought he must have forgotten it.

"Too bad," said Mr. Slingsby. "Well, let's see! Suppose we have some — er — Consommé

à la Périgord and some Béchamel aux Pollyop-
kins, and — er — Perquísites à la Tuberculosis —
and how would a little Eucalyptus with egg-
sauce à la Pajama do to end up with? You
could serve a simple meal like that without keeping us waiting, I suppose?" he inquired of the
landlord, in an airy, contemptuous tone.

When Mr. Slingsby had satisfied his soul
with torture, the landlord was the humblest of
created things. He compromised on ham and
eggs.

CHAPTER VIII.

OTHING had been said about it, but it seemed to be generally understood that, so far as money matters were concerned, Mr. Paul Brown had entire charge of the company's affairs. He found that he was looked upon in the light of the vanished Runyon — nay, more than this — he seemed to have become a sort of financial father to the whole Aggregation. Paul was not of an illiberal disposition, but he felt that the time was fast approaching when the line must be drawn in this matter. At Mr. Slingsby's suggestion he hired rooms for the entire company, but when he and Adèle went to their chamber to try to smarten themselves up a little before breakfast, he talked it over with Mrs. Brown, and they came to a very decided conclusion.

The breakfast was a long time in preparation; partly, perhaps, because most of the members of the company were drying themselves around the kitchen stove. Paul put his head into the kitchen and found all his friends there, socially steaming together. He made up his mind that he and Adèle would go out and dry on the sunshiny lawn between the tavern and the beach. Here, as they walked up and down, they were joined by Mr. Slingsby, who hailed them as cheerily as though the situation were an every-day experience.

"The modest meal," he remarked, "is well nigh ready. I 'ave procured access to the larder, and 'ave routed out a few humble viands to swell the bill-of-fare."

"Mr. Slingsby," said Paul, "I trust you will make our breakfast as satisfactory as possible in every respect, for when it is concluded we shall part company. Mrs. Brown and I have made up our minds to retire from the theatrical business. Mr. Runyon's departure has left certain responsibilities upon my hands, of which I shall endeavor to acquit myself. I will discharge our present indebtedness at this place, and I will put in your hands a sum sufficient to carry the entire company back to New York. After that, Mrs. Brown and I will resume our trip, which will necessarily take us in another direction. I have not the slightest doubt that an Aggregation of such talent as yours will readily find regular and steady employment in the city."

Mr. Slingsby stared hard at Paul for a moment; then he raised his right hand, and looked solemnly aloft.

"By 'Eaven's," he said; "The Prince of Jays! I knew he was too good to be true!" Then he grasped Paul warmly by the hand.

"Mr. Brown," he said, "your proposition does you infinite credit, and I shall be extremely happy to serve as your disbursing agent. I need not tell you, I suppose, how much I regret that we must sever?"

"You need not, Mr. Slingsby," replied Paul,

"but I trust you will allow me to assure you that Mrs. Brown and I have heartily enjoyed making your acquaintance and that of your friends, and that our brief connection has been of great interest, and, I may say, benefit to us."

"I am glad to 'ear it," said Mr. Slingsby. "I 'ave certainly tried to do my best by you. And, in reflecting upon this occurrence in future years, it will always be a great satisfaction to me that I 'ad 'old of you, and not an ignorant and unappreciative 'og like Runyon, who has not the

first instincts of a gentleman, and never knows
when it is time to let go."

And with a profound bow to Mrs. Brown,
Mr. Slingsby moved off. He had not gone far,
however, when a thought struck him, and he
returned.

"Under the circumstances," he said, with a
kindly smile, "it might not be amiss if we were
to garnish the occasion with a few bottles of such
wine as the country affords?"

"Certainly not," said Paul.

"Then we garnish," said Mr. Slingsby.
"My boy, you *are* a thoroughbred!"

The breakfast was served on the broad back
verandah of the tavern, overlooking the water,
and it was a very jolly meal, although ham and
eggs predominated in its composition. They
washed the ham and eggs down with champagne.
Everybody agreed that the practice of drinking
wine so early in the morning was improper in
the extreme; but they all drank it. Shipwrecked
people are entitled to certain indulgences, and
as Mr. Slingsby truly remarked, the champagne
which the landlord furnished was little better
than an inflated cider. So they ate and drank,
and felt happy that they were alive, and that they
were all such good people together; and after
a while a happy golden haze seemed to wrap the
whole party in a dreamy delight. When they
had finished, they pushed back their chairs and
sat contentedly gazing at the beauty of the river
under the morning sunshine. Then Mr. Slingsby
bewailed the fact that his fiddle was packed in
his trunk, on the wharf opposite the theatre, in
Tunkawanna. The landlord heard him, and

eagerly offered the loan of his own personal and
private violin. Mr. Slingsby loftily accepted the
offer, and when the instrument came, he began
to sing to them, in a pleasant, old-fashioned fal-
setto, a string of old-fashioned songs — sea-songs,
the most of them. He sang "Tom Bowling,"
"Wrap Me Up in my Tarpaulin Jacket," "Black-
eyed Susan," and other sweet, old, simple, silly
strains, while the golden haze grew more and

more golden, and some of the elder eyes grew
moist, and Aunt Sophy Wilks cried softly to herself, like a fat old child.

It was long past ten o'clock before they
finished their breakfast, and they would not have
finished it then if Adèle had not called Paul's

"When black eyed Susan came on board."
"O, where shall I my true love find?—"

attention to two facts: first, that the stage for
Tunkawanna and the New York train left at
eleven: second, that several of the company,
including Mr. Mingies and Mr. Weegan, were
expressing so warm an admiration for their present surroundings that they could not be contem-
plating less than a fortnight's stay.

After having been thus reminded, it did oc-
cur to Paul that his intimacy with those gentlemen
was increasing at an uncommonly rapid rate, and
that if he called Mr. Slingsby "dear old man" a
few times more, he would probably find the Brown
family tied for life, and, before they knew it, to
the wreck of Runyon's Dramatic Aggregation.
Still the golden haze enveloped his young head,
and Paul never knew exactly how he did succeed
in getting his eight friends off on the stage, which
presently lumbered up to the door of the inn. The
parting scene was very affecting. Every one of
the gentlemen privately borrowed ten dollars of
Paul; the ladies all kissed Adèle; then Mrs. Wilks
kissed Paul, and dropped a fat tear upon his cheek.
Mr. Mingies bestowed a fatherly salute upon
Adèle, and then the stage-driver interfered, and
with his aid, and that of the landlord and the
hostler, and a stray negro stable-boy, the eight
dramatic artists were finally stowed away in and
on various parts of the stage, and started off for
Tunkawanna to redeem their trunks, and to take
the train for New York. There was much kissing
of hands and waving of handkerchiefs, and, with
the best intentions, but somewhat inappropriately,
Mr. Mingies, in a deep bass voice, started the
chorus of "Good-night, Ladies," as they rolled
over the bridge in the morning sun.

The two Browns watched them from the back porch until they had crossed the bridge and swept into the high road. Then, just as they were turning away, Adèle gave a cry of astonishment.

"Look, Paul!" she said.

Paul looked. From a clump of bushes which the stage was passing, a tall man in a silk hat dashed wildly forth, with two other men in close pursuit. The tall man ran after the stage with a

speed that must have been born of desperation, unless he was a professional sprinter. He caught it, with his pursuers ten yards in the rear, and, grasping the baggage-rack, drew himself up, and was hauled to the top by Mr. Slingsby and Mr. Mingies. The other two men shouted to the driver, and one waved a bunch of white papers, but the driver appeared not to hear, for he whipped up his horses, and the stage rolled merrily around the corner.

It was Mr. Runyon

FTER breakfast, Adèle went to her room to lie down. She told Paul he had better lie down, too. Her advice was good, and perhaps Paul had better have followed it, but he said that he was not sleepy, and he thought the fresh air would do him good, and he would walk about the grounds a little.

He began by walking around the house, which he found a very interesting structure, for it was old and rambling. At one end there was a sort of shed-like roof extending over the driveway, and under this stood a tin-peddler's wagon, very neat, very new, and painted the brightest and most beautiful red that you can imagine. In the shafts stood a little sorrel mare, quite as neat as the wagon, but much less gaudy. He did not know exactly why he did it, but when Paul saw the wagon he sat down on a stone and regarded it attentively.

He had seen many red wagons in the course of his life, but it seemed to Paul, just at that moment, that that particular red wagon was far and away the prettiest red wagon he had ever seen. And it also seemed to him, at that particular moment, that a red wagon of just the right

sort was a singularly beautiful and desirable
object. He wondered who owned that wagon,
and whether the man knew what a good thing he
had in owning such a wagon. Paul had his
doubts about this. It took, he thought, a certain
delicacy of mind rightly to value a red wagon.
The owner was probably a soulless person, who
looked upon his possession merely in the light of
a wagon to which redness was incidental. He
felt that it would be a good thing in the interests
of abstract beauty, to rescue that red wagon from
such a man, who would, in all probability, let it
get muddy.

He had got to this point in his musings
when he happened to look up, and saw Adèle
seated at the window of her room, with her chin
upon her hands. She was gazing intently, even
rapturously, at the red wagon.

Then she, too, looked up, and their eyes met.

Her eyes were sparkling and her cheeks were
flushed.

"Oh, Paul," she said, softly, but he could
hear her quite distinctly, "how perfectly delightful

it would be to ride about the country together in
a dear little red wagon like that, and peddle those
delightful shiny tin things!"

Two hours, later a surprised tin-peddler and
a puzzled landlord went for the third time over
a large stack of bank-notes.

"Eight twenties, eleven tens and twenty-one
fives. Three hundred and seventy-five dollars,"

said the tin-peddler; "and every bill is good.
You can't fool me on money. Now, what in the
witherin' blazes do you make of it?"

The landlord cast a furtive glance at a great
tray of empty champagne-bottles, which a waiter
happened to be carrying through the room at that
moment. Then he engaged the tin-peddler's eye
with a look of profound thoughtfulness.

"Them theatrical folks is always kinder
queer and freaky," he said.

Chapter X

AUL and Adèle were perched on the high front seat of the little red wagon. Paul had his foot on the brake, and was carefully guiding the sorrel mare down a steep hill on the road that led from the inn in the direction away from Tunkawanna. Adèle held in one hand a piece of thin board, about the size of a school slate, faced with white paper on which were inscribed various strange figures and characters in red and black ink. This tablet she compared from time to time with some little slips of paper which she held in her lap with the other hand.

Paul looked hard at the horse, and his face wore an expression of gloomy thought — the expression of a young man from around whose youthful head a golden haze is rapidly evaporating, and who sees himself, through the fast-lessening mist, seated upon a red wagon, much like the rest of this world's red wagons, driving a sorrel mare possessed of few points beyond the generality of sorrel mares. But Adèle's face was undimmed by the slightest cloud.

"Is n't it perfect fun, Paul dear?" she said. "And *such* a relief! Of course they were all very nice, you know, and I am sure it was very interesting; but then, you know, of course it could n't last. And now I do feel *so* free and independent, don't you, dear?"

"O—eh—yes; why, certainly," assented Paul.

"The only thing I can't make out, Paul," said Adèle, "is how to get the *h* and the *z* part of this price-list right; and so long as I can't get that straight, of course it is perfectly impossible to make anything of the *n*'s and *x*'s."

"I am sorry, my love," said Paul; "I wish I could help you out, but of course I can't drive a new horse and study a complicated price-list like that."

"No, dear; of course not," said Adèle; "I beg your pardon. I did n't mean to worry you. We 'll wait till we get to that town — what did he say was the name of it? — where he said you could lay in supplies?"

"Brockham," said Paul. "Yes; we must get there before dinner."

Adèle's eyes were still fixed on the puzzling characters of the price-list.

"I hate to bother you, dear," she began; "but I do wish you would tell me if this can be possible. If *Hzz* on the dinner-pails means that they cost $1.02 a dozen, how can we retail them at two for five cents? And yet that certainly is what *Nx* means. And if *Nx* is right, then the soap dishes must be worth — let me see! — $3.25 apiece."

"I don't know, dear," said Paul. "I 'll work it all out when we get to Brockham."

He said this with something that sounded faintly like a groan.

"You are n't feeling ill, are you, Paul?" Adèle anxiously inquired.

"Oh, not in the least, I assure you," answered Paul.

"I should *hate* to have you feeling poorly just as we were going to have such fun," said Adèle. "How clever it was of you, Paul, to think of buying this horse and wagon!"

"I?" said Paul, with a little start; "I don't think it was my idea at all, my love."

"Oh, dear, yes!" said Adèle; "I could never have thought of anything half so bright. It was just an inspiration. Just like your thinking of this whole runaway·trip. Now, I never should have been capable of that."

"Oh, yes, *dear!*" Paul groaned in open desperation. Of course I do — only I — really, my dear, this horse makes me so nervous that I can't talk."

"Why did n't you tell me, dear? Of course I won't bother you for a moment. I 'll put away that wretched price-list, and I 'll just make out a little memorandum of the things we 've got to get at Brockham."

So she took out her little memorandum-book and her gold pencil, and began contentedly jotting down and figuring away. And as Paul watched her — which he could readily do, for, as a matter of fact, he was an old hand with horses, and a fearless driver — and saw how contented and happy the little woman was, and heard her humming bits of tunes softly to herself, his own spirits began to brighten, and he felt less self-reproachful. He certainly had bought, if not a pig in a poke, a horse in a golden haze; and most assuredly he and his wife were somewhat out of their natural place, seated upon the top of

a tin-peddler's wagon. But, after all, he reflected, the horse and the wagon were both good of their kind, even if they were not the magic outfit that they had seemed to him in a moment of enchantment; and as for being out of place, why, what was his object and his wife's at the present moment, but to get out of their natural place, and to get into somebody else's? Of course it was absurd, but evidently Adèle was happy, and if Adèle was happy, why should n't he be happy? and if they both were happy, why should they care about the absurdity of the happiness?

"Did you get the blankets down, dear?" he inquired, looking over Adèle's memoranda.

"Bless me, no!" cried his wife, with a merry little laugh. "I have put down sheets, though, and we shan't need sheets a little bit, shall we? People always camp out in blankets, don't they? And then I suppose our class of people use them all the time, any way, and do without sheets."

"Our class of people?" repeated Paul.

"Yes; tin-peddlers," Adèle explained innocently. And when Paul saw how deep a plunge his wife had made into her new identity, he promptly dived in after her, and immediately felt perfectly happy and quite at his ease.

"No more cigars for me," he said; "I'll buy a pipe at Brockham and smoke it. I used to smoke a pipe when I was working with Ernest — a stubby little brier-wood pipe."

"How delightful!" chirped Mrs. Brown. "Let me put it down: One brier-wood pipe, — Oh, Paul, how do you spell brier? I've got it b-r-i-r-e, and it does n't look right at all."

And so conversing, they came to Brockham.

Now, Brockham, from its name, you might take to be a solid old substantial English sort of place, a small city, perhaps; or, at least, a large town with an old manor-house concealed somewhere about its corporation. If you went to look it up in the Gazetteer you would expect to see Brockham put down something like this:

BROCKHAM.— County seat, Brockham County. settled abt. 1712. pop. 8,500. large woolen manufacturing industries. 8 schools, incl. Normal College. Pleasantly situated on w. bank Brock River chs. 3 prot. episc. 2 cong. 1 meth. 1 r. c. Brockham contains many fine residences, and has an interesting Revolutionary history.

That's what Brockham sounds like, does n't it? Well, Brockham was a country-store at a lonely crossroads near an extensive swamp connected with a small creek; an abandoned toll-gate, and the shopkeeper's weather-worn white house a hundred yards down the highway. That was all there was of Brockham, beginning and end and all, for it lay in the bottom of a valley,

and you could see over the level lowland for ten miles in every direction.

It was just noon when they reached Brockham and looked at each other in disappointment and surprise; for, without having said anything at all to each other, they had made up their minds as to what they expected Brockham to be, and it certainly was not anything of the sort.

On the verandah in front of the store sat a stout man in a chair tilted back, with his feet cocked up against a pillar. He was a pleasant-looking man, not a countryman; a business man from a large city, apparently, to judge from his well-kept appearance, his well-cut suit of tweed, and the well-trimmed mutton-chop whiskers that ornamented his otherwise clean-shaven face. He got up as soon as they came abreast of the store, stepped forward with an agreeable smile on his broad face, and gave them greeting.

"Good afternoon," he said; "let me hitch your horse. Here's a chain."

"Good afternoon, Mr. —— " Paul glanced up at the sign, — "Mr. Robinson."

"My name's not Robinson," said the stout man, genially; "Mr. Robinson's to dinner. I'm a friend of his, and I'm just tending store for him while he's away. Let me help your lady." And he gallantly handed Adèle down from her high perch. Then he turned to Paul.

"Guess Robinson's stocked up on tinware," he said, looking at Paul as if he were surprised that Paul should n't know it.

"Oh — oh — I — only — of course," stammered Paul. He had forgotten that he was a tinware peddler.

"The fact is," he explained, "I am not here
to sell to-day. I want to buy some things of Mr.
Robinson."

"Why, certainly," said the stout man.
"Might have known it; might have known it.
You 're in the retail line yourself, are n't you?
How do you find business?"

"Not very good," said Paul, who had recovered himself. And Adèle looked at him
admiringly.

. "Oh!" said the stout man. "Nice outfit
you 've got there. Been long on the road?"

"Not very," said Paul.

"Oh!" said the stout man again. "Nice
wagon you 've got there. May I ask who made
that wagon?"

"I could n't tell you," Paul answered him,
truthfully. "I bought it second-hand."

"Would n't have thought it," said the stout
man, in a complimentary tone. "Looks most as
good as new, don't it? Well, come right in. I 'll
see if I can hunt up Robinson."

"I thought you said he had gone to dinner," said Paul.

"May be he ain't got started yet," the stout man suggested. "Step right in, any way, and we'll see. Perhaps he's in the back shop. Come right this way."

The front shop was a large room nearly filled with every kind of merchandise. There were barrels of sugar and flour and oil, a hogshead of molasses, boxes of tea and coffee and rice and raisins and candles and all manner of things; there were calicos and flannels and fancy notions and boots and shoes and ribbons and cheap jewelry and chairs and mops and pails and tin and china-ware and hardware and agricultural implements and a couple of sewing machines and men's clothing and a few toys, and regiments upon regiments of canned goods arrayed in order upon the shelves. It was an interesting collection, and Adèle wanted to linger and examine it, but their stout friend ushered them through this palace of delights, and with a politeness that could not be denied, led them into the back room, over the door of which was a small sign: HAY, FEED, LIME, PAINTS, OILS AND PUTTY.

As they followed him, the stout gentleman, in his anxiety to be civil, thrust the door open so wide that it struck against a bag of meal on a shelf and sent a shower of dust over both of the Browns.

"Oh, *my* Gracious!" cried the stout gentleman in dismay. "Ain't I a big butter-fingers? I ought to have thought before asking the lady to come into such a place as this. I expect I've just about ruined your lady's hat. Step right back, and let me brush you off!"

They both assured him that it was of no consequence, but the stout man was distressed beyond measure, and insisted upon repairing the damage he had caused. He went behind the counter and procured a whisk-broom. Then he deftly aided Adèle to take off her jaunty Paris hat, and he proceeded to remove the last particle of dust from it, turning it over in his hands and flicking at it with his own white handkerchief, as tenderly as a young mother

might brush an excess of powder from the face of her first baby.

"My!" he said, "I would n't have had this happen for a farm, but I always was the awkwardest! My old mother used to say, when I was a boy, that some folks was all thumbs, but that I was n't even all thumbs — I was all toes. Well, well! Here, sir! Now I 've undone my mischief, as far as I can, for your lady. Let me see what I can do for you." And, in spite of all protests, he removed Paul's Alpine hat and carefully brushed it off, even to the under side of the rim. Then he went on to bestow the same care upon Paul himself, brushing him until he almost rubbed the nap off his coat.

"Got any down your neck?" he inquired, inserting his hand in Paul's coat-collar, and whisking the brush around as though he were a barber and had just given Paul a hair-cut. "There! I guess that will do."

They both assured him that it would do, but he continued his protestations of regret, until Paul, to put him at his ease, asked him if he could not show them the things they wanted to buy, without waiting for Mr. Robinson. The stout gentleman said he thought he could, and he proved to be a most active and obliging salesman. He seemed very much interested in their purchases, and surprised at some of them; but he did not transcend the bounds of polite inquiry, although the blankets puzzled him a good deal.

The prices at Mr. Robinson's store ruled low, and Paul was surprised to find how little he had spent when at last all their purchases were piled in a heap in the middle of the floor. But, as he gazed at the pile, he did not much wonder that the stout man was astonished at having sold such a bill of goods.

This is the list of the things they bought:

Three gray blankets,
Two red   "
Six cans of sardines,
One can-opener,
Three lbs. candles,
One can of axle-grease (the wheels of the wagon had squeaked.),
One wrench (the stout man's suggestion. It began to dawn
          upon Paul that when he bought the wagon he had
          not specifically included the fittings and other
          appurtenances in the purchase.),
One iron-kettle and one frying-pan ("so nice for camp-
          ing out," Adèle observed.),
One gross matches (suggested by the preceding pur-
          chase.),
One tin lantern (Paul had forgotten that he dealt in
          tin lanterns himself.),
One gallon kerosene oil (Paul's own bluff, after the
          lantern episode.),
One paper pins, assorted sizes,
Six papers needles,
Six spools cotton thread, Nos. 40—70,
One box paper collars (bought for curiosity.),
One pound molasses candy,
One nose-bag for the horse (stout man's suggestion
          again.),
One lady's veil (green barège was the fashion in Brock-
          ham.),
One Paisley shawl,
Two rubber overcoats,
Two knives and forks (Adèle reminded Paul that they
          had their own tin plates.),
One compass,
Two straw hats,
One quarter-pound pepper,
One bag salt,
One " hominy,
One " Indian meal,
One jug molasses,
One brier-wood pipe (at least it was a pipe, and it was
          made of wood.),
One pound cut-plug tobacco,
One bottle gargling oil (for man and beast).

The stout man helped them to load all the
things on their wagon, and with considerable
interest inquired their destination, and gave them
directions as to the best road to take. They had
been told to turn to the right at Brockham, and
to go a mile up the side road to a tavern, where

they could get their dinner, but when the stout man heard of this he strongly dissuaded them.

"It's a quarrymens' eating-house," he said, "and a pretty rough place. I would n't take the lady there."

"We might cook our own dinner," said Adèle.

"Of course you might," said the stout man, cordially, "and there's an elegant place to do it, in a patch of woods, under a hummock, about two mile up this very road."

So the stout man sold them some bacon and crackers (they ought to have thought of crackers before), and butter, and six eggs and a pint of milk, and a pound of tea and a pound of coffee, which they had also forgotten before, and two spoons, which came in the same category. And after Paul had remembered a feed of oats for the

horse, they bade each other good-by in the friend-liest sort of manner, and the Browns started up the road with their new possessions piled up on the top of their red wagon.

Before they had got as far as the white house they met a man coming along the road. It was undoubtedly Mr. Robinson, for there could hardly be another man in Brockham. It *was* Mr. Robinson. For when he saw the heap of what had lately been his property, on the top of the wagon, he stood stock still in wonderment, and then threw up his hands excitedly, and yelled to the stout man on the verandah of the store:

"Hi, there!"

But the stout man nodded back that it was all right, and Mr. Robinson, relieved of the fear that he had been robbed, but still wondering, went on toward his store, while the Browns jogged along the highway.

CHAPTER XI

THERE was not the slightest difficulty in following the stout man's directions. The road was straight, and the hummock he had told them of became visible — aggressively and almost impudently visible — before they had got half a mile on their way. It was not very much of a hummock, either, but it seemed to be conscious of the fact that, such as it was, it was the highest elevation for miles around, and it took advantage of the absence of real mountains to show off. It humped itself insolently against the sky, as if it said: "There ain't no hills here, only ME! There ain't no hills here, only ME!"

But when they arrived at its base they found it a friendly and pleasant sort of hummock, with a little patch of woods on one flank, and a spring in a hollow near by. The hummock itself was little more than a pile of round rocks, sparsely covered with turf and moss. On its bald top stood three lonely cedars.

"It 's a regular etching hummock," said Adèle; "just the kind they have in etchings. There ought to be some sheep on top — etching sheep, you know, with pin legs."

They turned into the patch of woods, unhar-

nessed the sorrel mare, and took the opportunity
of making her acquaintance. She seemed to be
quite a likable little animal, and, as Adèle remarked, she showed real intelligence in the man-
agement of her new nose-bag. Having cared for
the comfort of their horse, they took heed of
themselves, and with their kettle and sauce-pan
and some tin things from their own stock, including a tin pail which they filled with water from
the spring, and the provisions they had bought
at Brockham, they climbed to the top of the
hummock, where they found a bright little fresh
breeze blowing, and there they sat them down in
the shade of the big cedars, and cooked the first
meal they ever had cooked together.

The meal was, to use Paul's critical phrase
in summing it up, "splendid, but
spotty." They boiled three of the
eggs, and three they made into
an omelette. Paul made the
omelette, and it was very good,
for Paul and Ernest had had to
learn to subsist, often for weeks
at a time, principally upon omelettes
and crackers. But while they were making the
omelette they forgot all about the eggs in the
kettle. Now, a camp-fire kettle, as a rule, will
not boil much under an hour, and if you are
not firm and profane with it, it will sometimes
take an hour and a quarter. But they had put
the eggs in when they had put the kettle on, and,
out of the pure natural cussedness of kettles, it
boiled right up as soon as their backs were
turned. So, when they got to them, the eggs
were of the consistency of billiard balls; and

while they were discussing ways and means of
unhardening them, or at least of taking what Paul
called the Bessemer quality out of them, the
bacon which they had put on to fry got a little
burnt, and this did not improve its original musty
flavor. It was the kind of bacon that *will* not
crisp, but always lies limp, like a rat's tail. The
sardines, however, were excellent. On the whole,
they felt quite proud of their first attempt.

When they had finished, Adèle chose a
cedar and sat down with her back against it,
and Paul chose one opposite it, and sat down
with his back against that, and they chatted in
lazy comfort.

But Paul remembered his new pipe, and, although his cigar-case was not empty, he resolved
to begin without delay upon his pound of cut-plug.
Breaking in a new pipe is not the most pleasant
kind of smoking in the world. It's pretty sure to

try a man's temper, and it certainly tried Paul's.
Paul never got cross; but when his temper was
tried he did get stubborn. Later in the afternoon
he showed that his temper had been tried.

By degrees Paul dropped out of the conversation, but Adèle hardly noticed his absence,
for she was chirping away in childlike happiness,
and in perfect content with all the world, until
suddenly, as she gazed out upon the pretty landscape spread beneath them, a look of surprise
came into her face.

"Why, Paul," she said, "there's our stout
man! Where do you suppose he's going?"

"To his dinner, I suppose," said Paul, not
as pleasantly as he usually spoke.

"Then he will have to walk miles and miles
and miles for it," said Adèle; "for there is n't a
house anywhere in that direction."

It certainly did seem strange. The stout
man was walking straight across
the fields, heading apparently
in the direction of nowhere.
The two Browns followed
his course with interest.
Straight across the fields
he marched, until he
reached the road up
which he had told them
to turn. Here he climbed upon the top rail of
a fence and sat down.

"Paul," said Adèle, "I do believe he's
waiting for us."

"Then let him wait," said Paul. "No; on
second thoughts I'll accommodate him. He
probably wants to ask a few more questions of us."

"Well?" inquired Adèle.

"Well," said Paul, "he can ask."

And Paul buttoned up his coat, picked up the heavier cooking utensils, and started down the hill with a certain expression of stolidity and a fixedness of purpose about his walk and carriage which Adèle had noticed once or twice before, notably on the occasion when he told her that he wanted her to be his wife, and on another occasion when he told her that the twenty-seventh flat they had visited was the last one they were going to visit.

When they had washed up the "things" they harnessed the mare, who seemed quite glad to see them, and resumed their journey, discussing, as they gradually approached the place where they could see the stout man still awaiting them, a suitable name for their steed. They were hesitating between "Sorrellina" and "Tinnianna" when the fat man hailed them.

"Say," he called out cheerily, "give us a lift?"

"Why, certainly," said Paul, with his shoulders still looking uncommonly square.

"I ain't a tooth-pick exactly," said the stout man, as he climbed up with an agility that could hardly have been expected of him, "but you 've got a pretty broad seat here, and I guess it will *just* about hold three."

The seat proved to hold three, though not very comfortably, and the stout man could not help recognizing the fact.

"Kind of crowded, ain't it?" he said. "Well, well, I won't bother you very long — not if you 're the kind of people I take you to be.

Fact is," he said in a fatherly, confidential sort of tone, "I've been wanting to have a little talk with you two people ever since I set eyes on you. Would n't have thought it, would you?"

"Not in the least," said Paul, from between his shoulders.

"Thought not, thought not," said the stout man, looking first at Paul and then at Adèle, for he had settled himself between them, "but I *do*, all the same; and now I want you to understand before I begin, just to clear away any misunderstandings or doubts or suspicions or anything of that kind, that I'm your *friend*. Understand that? I ain't talking here in any capacity but that of a friend. I'm your friend," he said, laying one large hand on Paul's knee, "and your lady's here," and he rested the other large hand lightly on Adèle's knee; "and it's as a friend that I ask you to answer me just two questions — just two, understand. And if they seem to you im-

proper, why, don't answer them. But I think
they are such as one man may ask of another,
and in that light I would like to have you
answer them."

"If they are such," said Paul, "as one man
may, in my judgement, ask of another, I shall
certainly be most happy to answer them."

"Just so," said the stout man, pleasantly;
"in your judgement. Of course. Quite right.
If, in your judgement, they 're proper, you 'll
answer them. And if, in your judgement, they
ain't proper, why, you won't answer them. That
's the way I like to hear a man talk. Well, now,
question number one: What may be your name
and your lady's here?"

"My name," said Paul, "is Brown, Paul
Brown; and this is Mrs. Brown, Mrs. Paul
Brown."

"Just so," said the fat man, patting the
Browns' knees with the utmost friendliness; "just
so — Brown. Yes. And now — question number
two: What may be your trade, occupation or
profession?"

"You can see for yourself," said Paul; "we
are tin-peddlers."

"Thank you," said the fat man, with every
sign of gratification and pleasure in his face.
"That 's all I wanted to know, and I am much
obliged to you, sir, for the frank and friendly
manner with which you have met me half-way."

"You are quite sure," inquired Paul, "that
that is all you want to ask?"

"Quite," said the stout man, in his most
agreeable manner; "quite. There ain't another
question in the world I want to ask you;" and

he spread out his hands to show the completeness of his satisfaction. "And now," he continued, "though you have n't asked me, and although it may be of no interest to you, yet to put us, as it were, on an equal footing, I will tell you my name. My name is Bassett. Ezra P. Bassett. At least, that's my name up here, where I was born and raised; but when I am in New York, which is my place of residence, I don't use the Ezra in my business. I just call myself Bassett — Peter Bassett."

He looked from one to the other, as if he expected them to say something. But Paul only gazed calmly ahead over the landscape, and Adèle took her cue from Paul.

"My address in New York," continued Mr. Bassett, "is No. 300 Mulberry Street."

Then he paused and looked inquiringly from Paul to Adèle and from Adèle to Paul again.

Neither spoke. Mr. Bassett again laid a large hand on the knee on either side of him.

"That," he said, impressively, "is the Central Office."

"Mr. Bassett!" said Paul, "if my wife will excuse the profanity, allow me to say to you that we do not care a damn, not a damn, what your name is or where your office is, or whether it is centrally located or not."

"Of course not," said Mr. Bassett, still cheerful and agreeable; "of course not; but, of course, just as you reserved your judgement in your own case, and quite rightly, so I'm telling you what, in my judgement, I would like to have you know about me. I have told you that I am your friend, and that still holds good when I tell you further that my business is that of a detective, and I am attached to the staff of Inspector Byrnes, of whom you may or may not have heard. But understand me," and he settled his hands more firmly on the knees of the two Browns, "that it is not as a detective, but as a friend, that I am speaking to you now. And it is as a friend that I say to you: do not try to bluff me off nor to hold me off, nor to shove me off; but confide in me as a friend, and as a friend I will stand by you."

"Mr. Bassett," said Paul, "will you kindly tell me why we should confide in you, and why you should imagine that we have any occasion or any desire to confide in you?"

"Why, of course, of course," said Mr. Bassett. "Now, it's just this way: your name is Brown and your lady's name is Brown, Mrs. Paul Brown, and you are tin-peddlers."

"And why not?" asked Paul with a smile, but with his shoulders still squared.

"Because," said Mr. Bassett, "if you want to know why, tin-peddlers don't wear Dunlap

hats, nor their clothes ain't made to order by
Sullivan of Fifth Avenue, nor their lady's hats
ain't made by Madame Hortense. And because,"
the detective went on, growing more kindly and
genial with every moment, "I was onto you before you 'd got within a quarter of a mile of
Robinson's store, and I am onto you *now*. See?"

Paul smiled grimly.

"Mr. Bassett," he said, "your error is perhaps a natural one, but it is an error, neverthe-
less. My wife and I are not criminals, nor have
we done anything that could with any possibility
bring us within the province of the law. You
may be surprised to find us engaged in this
particular business, but if it suits us, and if we
have come honestly by it, it is nobody's business
but our own that we choose to engage in it. If
you have any doubt about that, I shall be happy
to go with you to the nearest magistrate and
prove to your satisfaction, as an officer of the law,
that I have purchased all that you see here as
honestly as I purchased the goods you sold me
some time ago. Or, if that will satisfy you, I
will show you the bill-of-sale here and now."

He made a move to take out his wallet, but
Mr. Bassett restrained him.

"I ain't got the first doubt of it," he said
heartily. "You 're a gentleman; I could see
that from the start. I ain't accusing you of
stealing tin-peddlers' wagons. You 're not that
kind; and, moreover, my young friend, I will be
perfectly honest with you. I won't try to bluff
you. I have n't the first idea in the world what
trouble you 're in; but I want to make you confide in me, that I may help you as a friend."

"I can assure you, Mr. Bassett, that we are not in any trouble at all, of any kind or description."

"I know, I know," said Mr. Bassett; "of course not. And I don't expect you to believe in me right at once. I know just how it is. I know just how you look at it. You say to yourself, 'this man here is a detective. It's his business to get people into trouble. He just wants to worm himself into our confidence, and then, when he has wormed himself in, he'll turn right around on us, and give the whole thing away. We'll keep our mouths shut and won't let him know anything' — that's what you say to yourself, is n't it? Of course, quite natural. That's the way that people who don't know anything about it think of a detective. They think he's all the time trying to get people into trouble. Well, now, my young friends, there never was a greater mistake. A good detective, who knows his business, gets more people out of trouble than he ever gets into trouble. You may not believe that, but it's true; and it's a credit to human nature that it is true."

"Is a detective's time very valuable?" inquired Paul.

"Sometimes it is and sometimes it is n't," replied Mr. Bassett, smiling affably. "Mine ain't, just at present, because I'm taking a vacation. But I'll tell you about that later on. I want to free your mind from this delusion you've got about detectives. Now, it's this way: you read in the papers about Detective So-and-so arresting a young man who's gone wrong, and that's all you think of. But, do you ever think," continued Mr. Bassett, bringing his fist down hard on Paul's knee, "of the young fellows who have gone wrong, that that detective *has n't* arrested? — that he 's taken from evil ways, that he 's rescued from desperate courses, that he 's stopped right on the ragged edge of suicide, may be, and restored to the bosom of their families? No, you don't; and why not? Because you don't know about it. There 's ten such cases to every one case that goes to prison. But the public never hear of them, and so they go about thinking that a detective ain't got any insides to him, and that his whole walk in life is to get nice young fellows into jail. Is that just to the detective? Is that Christian-like, I ask you? Is that kind?"

Mr. Bassett had become quite warm in his defense of the unfortunate detective; but his manner again grew persuasive as he recommenced.

"Then, moreover," he remarked, hopefully, "I 'll bet a hat, yes, sir, the best hat in New York, that you 're taking this thing altogether too seriously. You magnify it; you make too much of it. I know how it is with young people. They always think that any trouble they 're in is as big as all out-doors. They think there 's no getting over it; there 's no fixing it up. They don't know how experienced men of the world look on these things. Now, for instance, we 'll take a young man, say, who 's a little hard-pressed for money, and he borrows a few hundred, perhaps a few thousands from the old man's safe when the old man ain't around —"

"Mr. Bassett," interrupted Paul, angrily, "do you mean —"

"I don't mean anything, my young friend," responded Mr. Bassett. "I 'm just putting a case. Or, we 'll say he forgets to make a deposit to the old man's account in the old man's bank. Or,

we'll put it any way you want. Suppose he gets
in some way tangled up with the banking-system.
Or, perhaps he ain't tangled up with the banking-
system at all, and he's only married a lady —
an elegant lady, a perfect lady, but not *the* lady
that just suits his parents. Take any one of these
cases or any combination. He thinks, of course,
he's in a hole. But he ain't. If he had a friend,
the right sort of a friend — a discreet and experienced friend — who would be able to go to
the proper parties and talk to them in the proper
way, why, sir, he'd be out of that hole before he
knew where he was, and the public would never
be the wiser. And he'd have a more charitable
opinion of detectives all the rest of his life, that
man would."

Mr. Bassett looked earnestly from one to the
other of the Browns, with the expression of a fond
mother coaxing a three-year-old baby to tell who
stole the jam. Paul felt that it was impossible to
be angry.

"Mr. Bassett," said he, smiling, "I assure
you that if I were in any such position as you
seem to imagine, I should not hesitate to
make use of your ability and experience,
but — "

"You won't hey?" said Mr. Bassett.

"I won't," said Paul.

"Plenty of time," urged Mr. Bassett;
"you ain't got to decide hastily."

"Let us close the subject," said Paul, pleasantly, but firmly.

"I'd like to," said Mr. Bassett; "I'd like
to. But, you see, it don't lay in my power. I'm
a sworn officer of the law."

"Do you mean to say," demanded Paul, "that you are going to subject my wife and me to arrest because we 've refused to tell you the details of our private business?"

"Not in the least," said Mr. Bassett, always pleasantly. "I would n't treat a lady like that for any consideration, to say nothing of a gentleman. Not but what I could. If I was to ask at the next town to have you detained, detained you 'd be. You can stake your life upon it. If it was only on suspicion of being lunatics. But I don't propose to take any such course. All I ask is that you shall take time to reflect, for your own good, on whether or no you will let older folks guide you in this matter, and help you out of your troubles as older folks alone can do it. And that brings me," went on Mr. Bassett, "that brings me right to the point. As I told you some time back, I am taking my vacation up here where I was born and raised, and I am spending my holiday with my mother, who, if I do say it myself, and no man has a better right to know whereof he speaks, is one of the nicest old Quaker ladies you ever laid your eyes on. Her farm is just about two miles up this road; and there is no woman in the State can beat her on hot biscuit. Now she would be delighted, de-*lighted* to entertain you, your lady and your-self, — as guests, mind you, as guests, — while you think about things, and make up your mind what 's going to be your next move in this matter. There 's a nice place out on the front porch where your lady can sit and crochet, and there 's some real elegant trout-fishing in the creek behind the barn, and I can lend you a rod. A

man can think while he 's fishing just as well as
any other time."

Paul and Adèle exchanged glances. Mr.
Bassett smiled agreeably as he sat between them,
but he evidently meant what he said.

"I suppose," said Paul, "there is no alter-
native to accepting your kind invitation."

"Oh, yes," said Mr. Bassett, "you can drive
on to the next town."

"Under those circumstances," said Paul, "it
will give us great pleasure, Mr. Bassett, to avail
ourselves of your mother's hospitality."

CHAPTER XII.

R. BASSETT'S mother's farm-house was certainly all that the most exacting could ask, as a farm-house. It stood high up on the hill, looking southward over the valley, and it had red barns and stables, and back of the barns and stables was a most delightful little brook, that fairly chuckled "Trout, trout, trout!" at you as far as you could hear it. And, when Mr. Bassett's mother came down the flagged walk to meet them, they certainly saw a sweet, pretty old lady, with beautiful white hair and a pleasant smile. She did not wear the strict dress of the Friends, but had on a gingham that was neat, pretty and old-fashioned, like herself.

"This here is my friend, Mr. Paul Brown, and his good lady. Mr. Brown ain't certain whether he'll continue in the tinware business or not; and I have told him that I guessed you could put them up for a day or two while he's thinking about it. What do you say, Ma Bassett?"

"Thee's always welcome to bring thee's friends here, Ezry," said his mother; "and thee's assuredly brought two with good faces," added Mrs. Bassett, as she stretched out her hands to Adèle, and, after one look at her, kissed her in motherly fashion.

"My name's Lucretia; what does thee call thyself?"

"Adèle, Aunt Lucretia," answered Mrs. Brown, who had n't been born in Philadelphia for nothing.

Aunt Lucretia put her arm around Adèle's waist and led her into the great kitchen in the lean-to, that smelt of pot-herbs all the year

around, while Mr. Bassett and Paul went into
the stable to put up the horse.

"Your mother has a very pleasant farm here,
Mr. Bassett," remarked Paul.

"Pretty fair, pretty fair," said Mr. Bassett.
"Buckwheat here," he added, stretching out his
left hand; "corn here," stretching out his right.
"Wheat and rye down the road; cow-pasture
over the way; sheep-pasture up on the hill above
the woods; that's the old lady's kitchen garden
back there behind the house, and I'll show you
where the trout come in as soon as I can rig
a rod."

He gave one comprehensive sweep of his
big hands.

"From one son to another, father, son and
grandson, for three generations," he said proudly.
"And, young man, if it was n't my walk in life
to live in New York, looking after folks who get
into trouble and don't know how to take care of
themselves, I 'd be farming here, too. Come
along, sir," he said, as he led the way back to
the house, "and I 'll get you that rod. This is
just the kind of day when you 're likely to get
an elegant bite in a brook like that."

A broad hall ran through the old farm-
house, from front to rear, and on the walls of
this hall Mr. Bassett had hung his vacation-time
treasures. There was a small arsenal of shot-
guns, no less than six split-bamboo rods, and
more and queerer scap-nets than even the rods
accounted for, at which Paul gazed in astonishment until he caught sight of a mighty collection
of butterflies in a glass case.

"Interested in entomology?" queried Mr.

Bassett. " I do a little in that line, sometimes, myself. Bugs and trout — they somehow seem to go together."

Then they stepped into the kitchen, and, lo and behold! there was Mrs. Brown in a check apron, with her sleeves rolled up, and her arms deep in a pan of dough, which she was kneading under the directions of Mrs. Bassett.

" That's right," said Mr. Bassett, approv-

ingly. " Glad to see your good lady taking right a-hold, Mr. Brown. Make her feel to home, Ma Bassett. That's the way!" He exhibited the kitchen to Paul with pride in his eye, in spite of the humility of his language.

" Plain, but comfortable," he said; " plain, but comfortable, that's our style."

Then they went down to the creek; and there Paul had to confess meekly that he had never had a rod in his hand before. Mr. Bassett was as sincerely grieved as though Paul had owned up to entire ignorance of the Christian religion. But he at once proceeded to take this case of defective education in hand; and, before long, Paul could skitter a fly around for at least a minute-and-a-half without getting his line caught on the bushes. Mr. Bassett himself was a master-hand at casting. Hither and thither, among the most impossible boughs, over the raggedest thickets, among snags and driftwood, his fly danced about without a moment's rest. And, all the time, Mr. Bassett, as they whipped up the creek, enlivened their progress with an uninterrupted flow of professional reminiscences, being mostly tales of erring young people who either came to all sorts of horrible grief through contumaciously refusing to confide in a friendly detective, or, by so confiding, found themselves snatched out of the jaws of danger, and saved for lives of golden fortune and universal respect.

Then Mr. Bassett caught seven small trout, and Paul caught two, and Mr. Bassett said that that made "a mess," and they went back to the farm-house.

If you were a young runaway married couple who had been half drowned the night before; and had eaten a very indiscreet breakfast and a very inadequate and indigestible dinner; and had driven all day long over a dusty road in a wagon whose redness could not make up for its inadequacy in the item of springs, and you found yourself at the end of the day in the jolliest old farm-house that you ever dreamed of, with a dear old Aunt Lucretia to take care of you, and a most agreeable detective from the New York Central Office to tell you stories; if you had just eaten a glorious supper of brook-trout and crisp bacon, and three kinds of hot bread, and the best waffles in the world, with cinnamon and sugar on top of them, and cookies and oely-koeks and sweet pickles and cherry-pie and buttermilk; and if, after this meal, the agreeable detective had taken the male half of you aside, and unlocked a little cupboard near the chimney-piece, and introduced that male half to a bottle of such schnapps as the gold of the Indies could not buy in the Metropolis of the Western Hemisphere; and if, after all that, you strolled away, in a mild, sweet, fragrant Summer evening, when the insects were just chirping drowsily in the trees, and communed with yourselves as young married couples will — well, under these circumstances, you would probably come to the conclusion that you were doing pretty well, thank you, on the whole — would n't you? · That is the conclusion Paul and Adèle came to.

"How long do you suppose we *can* stay here, Paul?" asked Adèle.

"I don't know, my dear," answered Paul. "But if he 's waiting for me to confess to forgery or anything of that sort — well, you know we 've got a year to put in — a year less two days, tomorrow morning at six o'clock."

"Gracious, Paul!" cried Adèle. "It seems as if we 'd been away a year, already, does n't it? But if it was all like this it would be simply delightful."

"Well," Paul suggested, "I move we stay until they turn us out."

"I move we do, too," said Adèle. "But, oh, Paul, when we *do* have to go, remind me to get her receipt for those waffles!"

You are kindly requested to notice the growth of the first germ of home instinct in the breast of this young woman — a growth born of good waffles.

Then they stole back to the house, and, in the spacious old kitchen, Mr. Bassett and Adèle played backgammon; while Paul and the old lady chatted together: she telling him of her childhood days, when she had seen the Reservation Indians burning the hay-ricks in the valley, and dancing around the flames in all the gaudy horrors of their war-paint. And, meanwhile, the hired man, four dogs, two cats and a sick chicken slumbered placidly as near as they could get to the red-brick chimney-piece that held the shining black modern range.

And later on, Mr. and Mrs. Brown went to bed in a great high four-poster bedstead, in a great low dormer-windowed room. And, after they had chucked the feather-bed on the floor, they slept very comfortably.

Chapter XIII

HEY talked over the situation while they were dressing, next morning.

"Oh, m-m-m-m-vere," began Adèle, "I h-m-m-m-t-tell-m-m-M-f-s B-f-s-t — —"

"Take those hairpins out of your mouth!" commanded Paul.

"I beg your pardon, dear," said Adèle; "it *was* rude, but I only wanted to say that I had to tell Mrs. Bassett something about how we came to be here. I did n't tell her anything you would n't have wanted me to, I 'm sure, but when she asked me how long we had known her son, I thought I ought to explain just how he 'd met us, and — and —"

"Run us in?" suggested Paul.

"I did n't know what to call it," said Adèle, "so I just said 'invited.' And she was awfully nice about it, Paul. She did n't ask a single question, but only said she was glad we had come."

"Did n't she make any comments?" asked Paul, who began to wonder if Mr. Bassett often enlivened his vacations by buccaneering for guests.

"Not then, but a little later on, when we were talking about something else, she said — I wish you could have seen the corners of her mouth when she said it, Paul — she said: 'It's Ezry's trade to suspicion folks, and I sometimes think he's most too devoted to business.'"

"Was that all?"

"No; just before we went to bed, when she was helping me put away our things in the hall, she took up my hat and looked at it, and she said: 'I don't see what Ezry saw wrong about thee's bunnit, but if thee'd come in a bushel-basket or a golden crown I would n't have suspicioned thee.'"

"I guess the old lady's all right," said Paul.

"Paul, she's a *dear!*"

"So's Bassett," said Paul, remembering the

schnapps. "I mean, he's a first-rate fellow if you don't have to run up against him professionally. They're both good people; and they mean well, and they are certainly treating us royally. But, really, we can't stay here. After all, you know, if you come to think of it, it's a little bit of an imposition on our part. We can't go on playing suspicious characters for our board and lodging, even if Bassett did suggest it."

"No, of course not," said Adèle, as she

pulled aside the white dimity window-curtain and gazed out on the broad valley below them; all a pale, cool green under the light morning mist. "But it *is* so nice here! And so you 're going to tell them all about us, Paul?"

"I 'll be *hanged* if I am!" shouted Paul, with so much vigor that the collar-button which he was trying to put into place flew out of his fingers. "I 'm as good a man as Bassett, any day; and I don't propose to be bluffed by him or anybody else."

"But what *will* you do, dear?"

"Just go."

"But he 'll detain you — at the next town, don't you know?"

"No he won't. Yesterday, I think he would have detained us, but if Bassett is n't a fool — and I think he 's far from a fool — he 's had a talk with his mother by this time, and he won't say 'Boo' when we tell him we 're going."

"I suppose he 's afraid we 'd sue him for false imprisonment or damages or something, if he arrested us, and then they found out that we were n't robbers?"

"Hardly that," said Paul, doubtfully; "but then, people might have their opinion of a detective who could n't detect any more than that, with the chance he 's had."

"Oh," said Adèle, enlightened. "You think people would think it was a joke on him?"

"I think people might be inclined to regard it in that light," said Paul.

Paul's judgement proved to be correct. After breakfast — suppawn, (and that 's hasty-

pudding, if you 're not a Dutchman: Indian-meal,
what sinful folks call 'mush,') hot biscuit, flannel-
cakes, boiled eggs, salt pork, brawn, (that 's head-
cheese,) cornbread, apple-pie, fried hominy and
green tea — after breakfast Paul delivered his
little address to his host while they were inspect-
ing the cattle, which were Holstein stock.

"Mr. Bassett," said he, "there is no use in
our imposing ourselves any longer upon your
hospitality; nor is there any use in your concern-
ing yourself for our welfare. I 'm not going to
reconcile my present occupation with my choice
of a hatter, to please you or any man. But I can
assure you that the worst trouble I have ahead
of me is that of saying good-by to you and Mrs.
Bassett. And that, I am sorry to say, I shall
have to do to-day; for, as you may observe," and
he pointed to the red wagon, "I have a rather
large stock of tinware on hand, and I want to get
to work and peddle it off."

"Well, well," said Mr. Bassett, as he took Paul's hand and pressed it thoughtfully, "well, well, I am right glad to hear — not that you 're going away — I 'll be sorry for that, and Ma Bassett will be sorry for it — but that you 're going away without any *trouble* . . . or *worry* . . . or *apprehension* . . . or *alarm* . . . or unpleasant or disagreeable or inconvenient outlook of any kind *what — so — ever*." Mr. Bassett made this speech with great deliberation, and with considerate pauses, lingering on each suggestion of a possible cause for discomfort, as though he were giving Paul a last chance to seize on some word for a text for a full confession. But Paul confessed nothing, and Mr. Bassett sighed gently as he released his guest's hand.

"Well," said Paul, "I guess I 'll hitch up."

"No, no, you won't," said Mr. Bassett. "No; you won't do anything of the kind! Now that everything 's settled, and we ain't got any business on our minds, we 'll just go fishing. Tinware trade must be slack just now; most families must be pretty well tinned up, and you can just as well as not afford to take a few days off. You 've got the makings of a fisherman in you, and I 'll bring them out."

Paul felt obliged to decline this invitation, for he knew that he could not afford to trifle with the first glow of his enthusiasm in the tinware business. It was a tender thing, and might fleet away before his eyes. But he soon saw that it was a matter of delicacy with Mr. Bassett, and that his recent captor would esteem highly the favor of playing his host in a non-professional capacity. So he finally compromised, and agreed to stay to dinner, and to spend the morning whipping the trout-stream, with his entertainer. When this was settled, a pained look departed from Mr. Bassett's face, and they went after their rods.

After dinner — I do not think I will say more about their dinner bill-of-fare, except that it was bewildering — they found it very hard parting from their new friends. You see, these two young people had swung out of their own orbit, and had impinged upon a Home, and there was a great attraction set up right off, so that they hated to tear themselves away. There is a good deal of difference between a Home and the reddest of Wagons.

They had got their chariot out of the barn, and their sorrel mare hitched up, when Ma Bassett asked them to wait a minute, and she and Ezra went back into the kitchen. Paul was standing at the horse's head, and Adèle noticed a peculiar look come into his face. Now Adèle was the only person in the world who knew that Paul had possibilities of being mischievous, and she at once asked:

" Paul, what are you thinking about ? "

" I was only thinking," said Paul, " that I might ask Bassett if he wanted anything in the tinware line."

" You shan't do anything of the sort," said Adèle, " after they 've been so good to us. But I 'll tell you what you might do, and it would be *awfully* nice. Come here, I want to whisper to you."

Five minutes later Paul presented himself at the kitchen door, staggering under the burden of

a large assortment of tinware, selected by Adèle, of which he begged Mrs. Bassett's acceptance. And Mrs. Bassett after a while accepted it, and she gave him her blessing, while Mr. Bassett put a great package wrapped up in brown paper into the red wagon, and there was no end of good-byes, and then the Browns drove off up the dusty road.

It was a beautiful Summer afternoon, and their road wound its way up the hillside by easy grades. It was warm; but there were little refreshing puffs of breeze every now and then; and the two Browns sat up on their high perch and

enjoyed the day and the drive and their own
company and the slow, gradual, happy digestion
of their dinners. The little sorrel mare had com-
pleted the digestion of *her* dinner, and now she
tried to show that she felt her oats, and was duly
grateful therefor, by switching her tail, snorting,
and from time to time trying to introduce a sort
of skip, or hitch-and-kick combination into her
regular trot. But the tranquil condition of joy
which enfolded the Browns grew more and more

like simple old-fashioned slumber, until, late in
the afternoon, as the sun was beginning to settle
down in the western sky, Adèle suddenly gave a
nervous start, grasped her husband by the arm,
and gazed in his face with a look of horror.

"Paul," she cried, "do you know what we
've done?"

"N—No," said Paul, who was n't quite
awake yet; "I did n't know we 'd done anything."

"That's just it," said Adèle, impressively.
"What have we done? Nothing; absolutely
nothing."

"I don't understand you at all, my dear," said Paul, desperately puzzled. "First you say we have done something, and then you say we have n't done anything."

"Paul Brown," said Adèle, with tragic solemnity, as she held up the price-list before him and pointed with her fore-finger to the line:

"*Lxx* — 33 1/3 — 10 — 2, 1 off for cash *Zmx* net. 30 days."

"What did we start out to do? To sell tinware! At farm-houses! Now look there!"

She made Paul turn and look down the long expanse of gently sloping hillside up which they had been climbing all the afternoon. They could see the road back of them for miles and miles, bordered right and left by a continuous succession of thriving farms, every one of which might have contained at that moment some faithful housewife with a heart half breaking for a new outfit of tinware.

They gazed in silence, but Adèle's lips moved softly. She was counting.

"There are twenty-three of them," she said at last, "not including the flagman's little house at the railroad crossing."

"I don't think he'd want anything in our line," said Paul, snatching at a crumb of comfort.

"You can't tell," Adèle corrected him with severity. "He might want — a tin cup — or a cuspidor — we have both."

"Well," Paul suggested, somewhat feebly, "there are plenty more farm-houses left."

"They can never take the place of those farm-houses to me," said Adèle. "They are twenty-three opportunities lost, and something makes me feel *sure* that every one of them would have bought something. The very next house we come to," she concluded sternly, "you must sell them something, even if you have to sell it at a sacrifice. I don't mean to go to sleep to-night without saying we really have peddled."

Paul shook his head doubtfully.

"We are getting pretty near the top of this hill, or mountain, or whatever you call it," he said, "and I don't believe we'll come across any more houses until we get over into the next valley. I don't think anybody lives up here."

But Paul was mistaken. A turn in the road suddenly brought them in sight of a house, at least a sort of house — the sort of house that somehow always seems to get into picturesque situations on mountain-tops and in other desirable pieces of scenery — a perfectly plain, square, frame-house, with about as much architecture to it as a shoe-box stood on end. A thin, gaunt woman, with a forbidding face, sat in the doorway. She had a wooden platter in her lap, and was viciously hashing something. Paul objected strongly to making her his first customer.

"Anyone who would build a house like that

in a place like this does n't deserve to have tin," he said. "I don't believe that woman knows what tin is. She probably uses galvanized iron, or some such thing as that."

But Adèle would not listen to him.

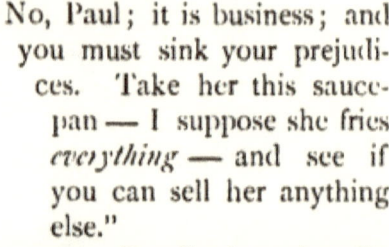

"No, Paul; it is business; and you must sink your prejudices. Take her this saucepan — I suppose she fries *everything* — and see if you can sell her anything else."

So Paul resignedly took the saucepan, and leaving Adèle in the wagon, marched off to the house. He was gone about three minutes. When he returned, his face was very red. He put the saucepan back in the wagon, climbed to his seat without saying a word, and started up the horse.

"What was the matter, Paul?" asked Adèle. "Would n't she buy the saucepan?"

"No," said Paul.

"What did she say, Paul?"

"She said she did n't want any saucepans."

"Was that all?"

"No," said Paul.

"What else did she say?"

"She asked me if I sold boilers."

"And what did you say?"

"I told her, 'yes.'"

"Well?"

" Then she asked the price."

" And you told her ? "

" Yes."

" And then what did she say ? "

" She asked me where I 'd buried the tin-peddler."

" Oh, Paul! What could you have told her ? "

" I told her correctly. I remembered about the boilers, because the price was marked on them. I said, 'fifteen cents.' "

" Oh, Paul, dear, will you never learn ? " cried Adèle. " Fifteen cents for a great big wash-boiler, the largest thing we have in the wagon ! "

" Big ? " repeated Paul, in a dazed way. " A boiler big? Why I thought—" here a sudden light broke in on him — " Great Scott, Adèle ! " he shouted, " I was thinking of *strainers*."

" Oh, you dear stupid boy !" said Adèle. " What a goose ! Well, you 'll have to drive back and explain to her. You can say you 're absent-minded, or something of that sort."

" My dear," said Paul, " I would n't go back and face that woman again for all the tinware in the civilized world ! "

CHAPTER XIV

THEY drove on for ten minutes before Paul spoke again, evidently at the end of a long train of thought.

"Now, Bassett," he said, just as if Adèle had been following him all the time; "Bassett would never have done that. Mr. Bassett certainly had his suspicions, there's no use denying it. But he knew I was n't a horse-thief."

Adèle smiled behind her hand to see the conqueror of the mighty Bassett thus cast down by a lone lorn woman.

"My dear," she said, "*nobody* in the *world* would take you for a horse-thief. That old creature has probably lived up here all alone until she is half crazy."

This reflection seemed to cheer Paul up immensely; and, being reminded, by the mention of the name of Bassett, of the fat parcel that their late hosts had given them, they hauled it forth and examined it. It was a characteristic Bassett bundle. Its big folds contained four Spring-chickens deliciously broiled, several kinds of pie, some dairy-cheese and pot-cheese, slices of cold ham, a little bottle of mustard, a paper "screw" of pepper and salt, and a small flask of the unapproachable schnapps.

The realization of the fact that they were

hungry, which somehow came to them with the sight of these good things, brought them face-to-face with another exciting and interesting truth —they were about to camp out for the first time, and to sleep in their own wagon. This put them suddenly into a new flutter of life. Speaking in a general way, their situation was admirably adapted to this end; for, as Adèle remarked, there was n't a soul within miles, except the old woman, if she could properly be called a soul. The only thing they had to do was to find water, for they had quite forgotten to bring any with them. Fortunately, they were not long in discovering a little creek, almost dried up, but with a thin thread of water still trickling among the hillside rocks. Near by there was a patch of dry mountain grass, where they tethered Sorrellina or Tinnianna — for the choice of her name still hung in the balance. They would have liked to push on to the top of the hill while it was yet light, but, as the little creek rose in a neighboring bog, they concluded that it was best to stay near the base of supplies. So, when the animal with the glut of names had been made comfortable, they began to build their fire. This was rather a tedious operation, for there seemed to be very little dead wood. Paul might have cut some fat pine knots, but he had forgotten to provide himself with a hatchet or a saw, when he was sampling the stock of Mr. Bassett's friend. His entire tool-chest consisted of a can-opener and a monkey-wrench, and was frankly and shamelessly inadequate to the situation.

Paul's back was beginning to ache with stooping down, when he heard Adèle call him. She had climbed to the top of a little rocky eminence somewhat further up the mountain-side, and there he followed her.

"Oh, Paul!" she said; "if we could only have *that*, how it would burn!"

She pointed to a large sign, made of boards that had once been neatly painted, but now so sun-scorched and weather-beaten that it was not quite easy to make out the lettering, which was as follows:

DESIRABLE BUILDING LOTS
and
ELEGANT VILLA SITES.
LOCATION UNSURPASSED —
ALL MODERN IMPROVEMENTS.

"But, of course," she went on, "it belongs to the owner of the lots, and so we must n't touch it."

"It is a living lie," said Paul. "Stand aside, my dear."

He raised a large round stone above his head, and sent it crashing down upon the sign. Then, silently and firmly gathering up the splintered fragments, he bore them to the creek-side,

and in five minutes the poor old sign was expiating its iniquity in dancing flames. Then they made tea, and fried a little bacon, just for the sake of frying something; and, after they had made an excellent meal, they sat down with their backs against a boulder, Paul to smoke his pipe, and Adèle to give him a lesson in the price-list.

But the pipe was beginning to grow black and sweet and highly enjoyable; and the price-list had long ceased to be anything but the abomination of desolation mentioned in the scriptures, and by-and-by they contented themselves with simply sitting there and watching the sunset, which was making a series of beautiful transformation scenes away down at the lower end of the valley.

Their camping-ground was a little above the winding road up which they had been traveling, and they looked down upon it as they sat against

the rock. It was a lonely road, narrow and ill-
cared for, and they were greatly surprised when
they saw a curious little figure climbing up it.
Adèle drew a little closer to Paul.

"Oh, Paul!" she whispered; "it can't be —
tramps!"

"I think not," said Paul; "in fact, I am
sure. It's only a boy, and he's carrying a
bundle."

But Adèle continued to look rather nervously
at the dark figure until it came fully into view in

the bright sunset light. Then she gave a little
sigh of relief and an apologetic laugh.

"How absurd!" she said. "Why, it's only
a little Italian boy — and, oh, Paul, dear, do look
at what he's carrying!"

The boy was a brown-skinned youngster,
thirteen or fourteen years old, with dark, curly
hair; and he was bent almost double under the
weight of a great burden of tinware which he carried on his back — a poor little outfit compared

with the Browns', but still a heavy load for a half-grown boy to carry. Yet he trudged cheerily along, whistling and keeping step to his own music; and, as he passed them, he hailed them in a happy childish voice:

"Buona sera!"

"Buona sera!" Paul answered him. And, as the little figure vanished up the road, Adèle called softly after him:

"Buona sera!"

But, as he passed on, they turned to each other with troubled faces.

"Oh, Paul," said Adèle, "was n't it pitiful? Such a load, and yet such poor little wretched things!"

"Yes, *by Jove!*" said Paul, knitting his brows.

Then they sat in silence until the light had almost faded from the western sky.

"Oh, Paul," said Adèle, at last, with a long-drawn sigh and a shake of her little head, "I am *so* thankful we forgot those farm-houses!"

"Well, dear, we must go to bed," said Paul, after a long silence.

"Yes; in our wagon!" said Adèle, brightening up, for the little Italian boy had really weighed heavily upon her mind. "Oh, Paul, won't it be fun!"

And they very soon forgot their small competitor in the tinware business, for they found that going to bed in the wagon was quite a complicated and protracted piece of work. In the first place, they had to take all their stock out of the wagon in order to get in themselves; and then, when the stock was all out, they remembered the

evening dew, and were obliged to consider that
the tinware would surely rust if it were left all
night on the damp grass.

However, by this time they had grown quite
fertile in expedients, and, the night being warm,
Paul took one of their blankets and fastened it
by each of its four corners to the wagon-springs.
Into this he piled all of their stock, and over this
again he spread another blanket, and so tucked up
the tinware for the night. They had now three
blankets remaining, and two of these Paul spread
on the floor of the wagon, keeping the other to
cover them. Then Adèle climbed into the hollow
box of the wagon to see how she liked their new
sleeping quarters.

Her report came out to Paul with a hollow,
booming sound, as though she were lost in a
distant cavern. She said, first, that it was dark;
and then she said that it was too hard for anything. So she climbed out again, and Paul proceeded to despoil the tinware of its upper blanket.
Adèle tried it once more, and said that it was

better, but that she wished they had thought to get a mattress. Then they both climbed in and tried to settle themselves for the night.

But Adèle had a tender conscience and a deep sense of responsibility.

"Paul," she said, "I can not sleep while I think what would happen to that tin-ware if any dew got on it. I do wish you 'd try and think of something else to do with it."

So Paul got up somewhat reluctantly, and devised another expedient. This time he piled all the tinware on top of the wagon, over their heads, and covered it with its blanket.

"Oh, thank you, dear!" said Adèle, when he came back.

"You 're entirely welcome dear," replied Paul, but hardly in his very pleasantest voice. "Do you think you could get just the least little bit over that way?"

"I 'll try, dear," said Adèle; "but there is n't very much room, you know. Are you going to shut the door, Paul?"

"I can't, dear," said Paul; "somehow my feet seem to stick out."

"I 'm so sorry, dear," said his wife. "Do you suppose we could have an extension put on?"

"A — what?" said Paul, sleepily. "I tell you they 're too *long*."

"I did n't mean your feet, dear," said Adèle. "I meant an extension to the wagon."

"Oh, yes!" Paul groaned; "certainly — just as you please, my dear — in the morning."

Then they tried to sleep. But the floor of the wagon had something to say about that. It made itself felt even through three thicknesses of blanket, and it proved to be a singularly hard, unyielding floor. Paul drowsily wondered if he could n't some time have it taken out, and a spring-board substituted. He was just sleepy enough to make this plan seem quite feasible, and he turned over on his back to think of it more comfortably. In doing so his elbow landed heavily upon his wife's head, while at the same time he thrust her violently against the side of the wagon.

"Oh, Paul!" cried she, "you 're *killing* me! How could you be so cruel? And just as I was getting off to sleep so nicely, too!"

This last clause was a fib. But the best woman in the world, when she has got a man down, *will* rub it into him. Paul apologized profusely, but not in a very clear or connected manner. Then he tried to efface himself against his side of the wagon, and he only gave a subdued moan of pain when, shortly after, Adèle plunged both her French ·heels vigorously into the small of his back.

It was now Adèle's turn to apologize, and she felt so badly about it that she not only set forth her regrets at great length, but made Paul wake up to be sure that he understood how badly she *did* feel. And having once waked up, they lay awake and talked it all over. They came to the conclusion that they did not *altogether* like sleeping in the wagon as it was arranged at present.

"If," Adèle said, "it only had a spring bottom —"

"And a tail-board to let down for my feet," suggested Paul.

"And a little more ventilation —"

"And about two feet more width —"

"And if it did n't smell quite so much of the things we put in it — why, Paul, I can smell sardines, and bacon, and pepper, and tobacco, and axle-grease, and kerosene oil, and I don't know how many other things, all at once."

"If we 'd built the wagon in the first place," said Paul, "it would have been all right. But I don't believe that man ever slept in this wagon."

"The wretch!" Adèle exclaimed. "Did n't he tell you he did?"

"Well, no," said Paul, "now I come to think of it, he did not. I asked him if I could sleep in the wagon, and he said I could if I bought it."

"Oh!" said Adèle.

They gave it up after a while, and decided that they did not really care about making a bed-chamber of their vehicle until certain radical faults in its construction had been remedied. They thought they would get up and take a little walk to stretch their legs and limber up the many sore points which sprang into life all over their frames.

They crawled painfully out of their box,

and, when they had got out into the open air,
they were astonished to find how large and cool
and generally delightful the world was. The
moon shone so brightly that, for a moment, it
seemed as if they were standing on a snow-clad
hill near the shore of a broad white lake; for a
great mist filled the valley below them, and
buried in its cloudy depths the fields and farms
and woodlands.

"Oh, Paul," cried Paul's wife, "how beautiful! I am not sleepy now, or even tired. Are
you? Let's walk to the top of the hill and look
down. It must be like getting into heaven to
see it all from there!"

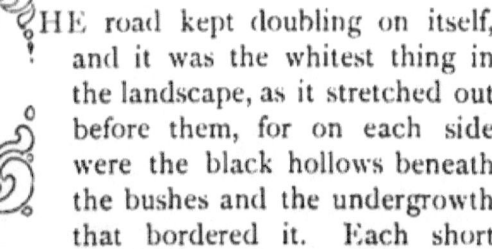

CHAPTER XVI

THE road kept doubling on itself, and it was the whitest thing in the landscape, as it stretched out before them, for on each side were the black hollows beneath the bushes and the undergrowth that bordered it. Each short ascending reach lost itself in the darkness; and, though they could not have told why, it gave them a strange sort of quick, surprised pleasure to come around the turn and find that silver path leading them in just the opposite direction, and yet ever tempting them upward with its wayward beauty. At each turn they knew what they were going to find, and yet each time it was a surprise; and the road kept the best surprise of all until the last; for suddenly they came around a thicket, and there it lay before them running straight up, and over the bare brow of the hill, as if it run into the hollow of the sky. Paul felt Adèle's hand fall upon his arm, not in affright, but as though she cautioned him not to break the silence.

" Look, dear," she said very softly, pointing to the side of the road.

The little Italian boy lay there, stretched on his back, with one arm under his head and his

other hand clutching at his ragged shirt and
pulling it open at his brown chest, that rose and
fell in his sound, child-like sleep. His lips were
relaxed in a babyish smile, and the dew glistened
like frost on his curly black hair. Adèle gazed at
him until the little picture blurred and wavered
through tears. She slipped her hand into Paul's,
and he pressed it hard.

They turned back a little, and sat down on
the stones by the roadside.

"Paul," said Adèle, after a long while, "do
you know what I'm thinking of?"

Paul nodded. "Give him something!"

"Yes; give him a whole lot of things. And
bring them up here, don't you know, while he's
asleep, and leave them for him to find when he
wakes up. Would n't that be lovely?"

"First-rate," said Paul.

"Oh, you 're such *a dear*," whispered Adèle, "to think so, too. But then, I knew you would. Now, what shall we give him?"

"A blanket, the first thing, I should think," said Paul.

"Yes; of course," Adèle said; "you 're always so thoughtful, Paul. And what next?"

Paul ruminated.

"'Nother blanket," he said at last.

"I meant tinware," Adèle explained.

"Oh!" said Paul. "Well, give him the wash-boiler. I would n't put that thing to bed another night for a farm."

"It 's a nice wash-boiler, Paul," said Adèle reproachfully; "and you ought n't to feel angry with it because you got it mixed up with a strainer. Besides, the poor little fellow could n't carry it."

"Well, if he won't take it any other way," said Paul obstinately, "give him the horse and wagon to carry it."

Then their eyes met. The same thought came to both at once. It was born in a jest, but it trembled into earnest before they knew it; and there they sat looking at each other and silently talking, with no need of speech to make each other understand. It was Adèle who first spoke aloud.

"Oh, Paul! do you think we really might —?"

"Why not?" said Paul. "After all, what did we come out for except to have a good time? And I 'm not so stuck on that wagon as I was."

"Oh, Paul, I won't let you say that!" cried

Adèle. "You wrong yourself — you were n't thinking of that at all. We were having a lovely time with the wagon, if it *was* horrid to sleep in. But then it would have to come to an end sometime. And I 'm sure *he* 'd have an ever so much better time with it, and it would mean a great deal more to him than it would to some man who could afford to buy it from us."

"Well, I 'm game," said Paul, cheerfully. "It won't leave us with much ready cash, but then I suppose we can load up again."

"You don't mean to say," Adèle exclaimed, somewhat horrified, "that we 've spent all we had when we came away!"

"Pretty near," said Paul; and then he smiled at her shocked face. "You must remember, my dear, that we 're only experimenting, so far. When we find out what we really want to do, we can begin to economize."

This explanation greatly relieved Adèle's soul.

"Oh, yes, of course!" she said; "and we can economize on ourselves; and then what we do for other people will be a luxury. That will be nice, won't it?"

Anything that was nice for Adèle was nice for Paul.

"Let 's wake the little beggar up and tell him about it."

"Oh, Paul, how can you think of such a thing?" said his wife, holding up her hands. "Of course it 's got to be a *surprise!*"

"Why, how on earth," inquired Paul, "can you surprise a fellow with a horse and wagon? You can't slip it in his pocket, or put it in his stocking."

"Don't be absurd, dear," his wife said rebukingly, "and I 'll tell you just what we 'll do. You 'll make out a deed of gift, or whatever you call it, and we 'll stick it in his pocket — "

"He has n't got a pocket," interrupted Paul, "any more than he has socks."

"You know what I mean, Paul, perfectly well. Let 's come right along and do it."

So Paul obediently came along, and they retraced their steps to the camping-ground.

For one moment, as they gazed at the embers of their camp-fire, in which a little life yet lingered; at Sorrellina (or Tinnianna,) waking from her placid dreams to cast a look of friendly inquiry toward them; at the tinware cosily put to bed under its blanket, and at the wagon, which, even under the moonlight, retained something of its peculiarly red redness — for one moment a pang smote them both at the thought of giving it all up; but they did not falter.

Adèle began to pack their own personal hand-bags while Paul got out his bill-of-sale, and started out to make a transfer in something calculated to suggest a legal form. But here, at the very beginning, he struck upon a snag.

"I 'm afraid, my dear," he said, after scratching his head in silence for a while, "that I 've got to wake that little cuss up. How the deuce can I transfer this thing to him if I don't know his name?"

Adèle knit her brows in thought.

"Could n't you write it so badly that nobody could read it? and then they could n't say it *was n't* his name, you know."

"I might do that," said Paul; "but there

ought to be enough of a name for him to recognize himself by."

"That's true," said Adèle. "I don't see how we're going to get around that."

"I'll tell you," said Paul. "Don't you know what an everlasting lot of names those foreigners always have? Well, let's give him all we can think of, and then we'll be pretty certain, among them all, to strike on the right one."

So they made out the transfer with all the Italian names they could think of, ending with an

illegible scrawl. Some of the names they put in, not at all because they thought they might belong to the boy, but because they sounded pretty.

This is what the result of their collaboration looked like:

When they had finished, they regarded their work in admiration.

"I always *was* a bad writer," said Paul, proudly.

"Yes, dear," said Adèle, very much pleased; "but I never thought you could write as badly as that."

Paul put the tinware and the stores back into the bedroom. As the moon went down, he was obliged to light the lantern, which added a gypsy-like attraction to his work, and he dawdled over it until Adèle was obliged to remind him that the sun would be up if he lingered much longer.

But the eastern horizon was still cold and gray, and the moon had not faded in the sky, when they drove the mare up as near to the place where the sleeping boy lay as they thought they could safely advance without waking him. There they tethered her, warmly blanketed, and up the road they went and found the boy still sleeping. He had scarcely moved since they left him.

Adèle had written a little note in such Italian as she had learned — and taught — at Madame Chambray's school, to explain the situation, and to advise him as to the moderate and appropriate use of such portion of his new name as he might find convenient for business purposes. And if any one were to endeavor to take his property from him, he was to address Mr. Parkins, at the nearest of the banks of deposit where Paul had provided a *cache* for that creature of his own imagination.

Then they went back to say a last farewell to the outfit that had been theirs; and Paul patted Sorrellina's neck, and Adèle stroked Tinnianna's nose; and that team of one single horse ate of a bush, and manifested no emotion.

There was nothing left now but to give Paolo Etcetera his little packet of papers, which they had tied up with the price-list. Paul stooped down and slipped it under the grimy hand that lay upon the brown breast. The small fingers

slightly closed upon it, and the boy breathed the light sigh of contented sleep. Adèle knelt down by his side.

"Paul," she whispered, "do you think I'd wake him?—"

"No," said Paul; "a child who could sleep like that must be built like a time-safe."

Adèle bent over and kissed the boy's forehead. Then she rose, and they went on their way over the brow of the hill, where another valley lay at their feet.

"I wonder—" said Paul, dreamily.

"What dear?"

"What in thunder he'll make of the price-list," said Paul.

"Oh, Paul," said Adèle, "please don't joke!"

CHAPTER XVII.

IT seems an easy thing to make a spring-board, run up it, and dive off into the deep water of a pleasant swimming-place. Any boy can tell you how it is done. You go to the saw-mill, shortly after the foreman has gone home to dinner, and ask permission of the back-door to take a nice, long, springy plank, with considerable "lift" to it. Then you lug it down to the water's edge, and you cock it up over a big round stone, at the proper angle over the water, and hold the shore end down with a big flat stone. Then you just stand back, take your run, and dive.

Yes. And there is a point in that run when you become conscious that you are made in two parts, and the front part of you is collapsing and tumbling right in on your rear elevation, which seems to be composed principally of air; and cold, very thin air, at that. You know you have

got some pores left — several billion of them —
for they are all pricking, especially those in the
place where your hair used to be. Otherwise
there is nothing solid about you, except a chok-
ing sensation in the throat and head, and a
feeling of about-to-be-brokenness all the way up
your spine. That 's the point where you go back
and say you did n't get the right kind of run on ;
and the other boys say: "Ah, 'fraidcat !" And
then you run and dive, somehow. You would
dive off the Rock of Gibraltar to cool off the red
feeling in your cheeks.

Paul Brown had never had any experience
with spring-boards at swimming-places, but he
was getting the same outfit of sensations as he
walked down the broad, shady main street of
Greenhill Plains, on his way to the Greenhill
Bank, where he was going to cash Mr. Parkins's
first check.

Paul had prepared an excellent spring-
board. He had made a deposit for Mr. Parkins,
and he had constructed a signature for a key to
that deposit, and he had notified the people of
the bank that Mr. Parkins, in his wanderings in
search of health, was liable to drop in on them
at any moment, and to check against his deposit.
And here he was in Greenhill Plains, and the
Greenhill Bank was down the street, and nobody
but his wife, who was at the Ontowasco House,
and he himself, knew that he was not Mr. Parkins, but Paul Brown. And only he himself knew
that he was not even that — he was Paul Brown
in a blue funk.

It had all seemed so simple — to walk
pleasantly and naturally into the bank, and to

say to the Cashier: "Good morning, sir. How do you do? Allow me to introduce myself — Mr. Parkins, of New York. Beautiful town you have here — beautiful!" Then the Cashier was to say: "Mr. Parkins? Oh, yes! Mr. J. P. Parkins? Glad to see you, Mr. Parkins. What can I do for you this morning?" But now that the time had really come to do it, somehow all the simplicity went right out of the scheme, just as the jump goes out of the boy on the spring-board.

For the first time in his life, Paul was about to pretend to be something and somebody that he was not. For the first time in his life he was about to sign a check with a name that was not his, and to which he had no legal right. And the moment the last letter of that signature was formed, Paul Brown would belong to a class of men whom he had looked down upon all his life — the class of men who have "*alias*" after their names. Paul Brown, *alias* J. P. Parkins! And if it ever were discovered, how could he explain to all the great world that reads newspapers that he had put on that criminal's mask for no evil purpose?

He cast up his eyes, and saw that he had come to the bank. It was only a small red-brick building, and nothing in any way formidable, but Paul hurried past it as if it were the mouth of the cave of the Giant Despair. He went a few yards beyond the bank, and then he turned and re-traced his steps, trying to get something like a determined sound into the soles of his shoes. This time he got a few yards beyond the bank in the other direction. He felt that he must put an

appearance of naturalness on this last promenade,
so he turned abruptly in a cigar-store and asked
for a cigar.

"What price?" inquired the clerk.

"Oh," said Paul, "about twenty cents."

He was not looking at the clerk, but he felt
that the clerk was looking at him, and in a very
peculiar manner. If he had ever smoked the
cigar that the clerk sold him for twenty cents, he
might have understood why the clerk's manner
was peculiar. But he never smoked the cigar.

After this there was nothing to do but to
go into the bank, and he went, thanking his stars
that the day was warm enough to account in
some measure for his general appearance of high
fever.

Now, Paul had selected the Greenhill Bank
as a depository of his traveling funds because he
had found that it was rated at the mercantile
agencies as a small, but old, sound and respectable institution. Greenhill Plains was an old and

well-known town, and he had thought that it was one that would probably support a thriving, well-established bank, wherein a strange deposit would attract no special attention. He did not know that Greenhill Plains was not only an old town, but what might be called a senile town, whose affairs had been at a stand-still for several generations; and that the one small bank of Greenhill Plains did little more than a petty money-lending business, as agent of larger institutions in other cities. Its only depositors were, so to speak, the local butcher, baker and candlestick-maker, and among theirs, Mr. Parkins's new account shone like a diamond in a handful of bird-shot. But, as I said, he knew nothing of all this.

Paul was too nervous when he presented himself at the Paying Teller's window to take much notice of his surroundings; and, indeed, there was nothing to see, except the usual interior of a small country bank — a room divided lengthwise by a counter surmounted by a net-work of stout wire. The wire net was pierced with the two little windows which we may see in every bank — the one through which the Receiving Teller is condescending, and the one through which the Paying Teller is rude. On the one side of the railing were desks and stools, the big safe, and the one bank-official in sight — a large, gaunt, aggressive-looking young man with a prominent chin and a mouth that would have been very useful to a retriever. On the other side of the counter were Paul, two chairs, two spittoons and the *Bank Note Detector* on a broken file. At the back of the room was a half-glass door, marked " Private Office."

The bank clerk was sitting on a high stool, writing in a large book. He paid no attention whatever to Paul, until the latter, after fidgeting for a few moments, began:

"I — I — I beg your pardon —"

Then the bank-clerk turned slowly, looked at Paul with anything but a pleasant expression, turned back to his work, and slowly added up two long columns of figures. Then he carefully descended from his stool, walked to the window, and said: "Well!" so abruptly that it made Paul start.

"I — I 'm Mr. Parkins," began Paul, feeling all the blood in his body go suddenly to his head, but still conscious of an inexpressible sense of relief that the fib was positively told.

"Well?" said the bank-clerk again, still more disagreeably than before.

"Mr. J. P. Parkins," said Paul.

"Well?" said the bank-clerk, so impatiently that Paul hastened to stammer on.

"I 've got some money here," he said.

"So 've other folk," said the bank-clerk, curtly.

"I 'd like to draw about two hundred and fifty dollars," said Paul.

"How much?" the bank-clerk asked sharply.

"About two hundred and fifty dollars," said Paul, feebly.

The bank-clerk regarded him with a more stern expression than any he had so far assumed.

"Do you know," he demanded severely, "*how much money* you want to draw?"

This time Paul managed to say two hundred and fifty dollars. The clerk gave a sort of snort.

"Where 's your check?" he asked.

"I have n't drawn it yet," said Paul. "I—"

"Where 's your check-book?" the bank-clerk interrupted him.

"It 's here," said Paul, producing it.

The bank-clerk gave him his instructions in a voice so loud that any one passing in the street must have heard every word.

"Take that pen and ink there," said the bank-clerk, "and write out a check for the amount you want. Put the amount in writing on this line, and the figgers down there, and your name here. Top line 's for the date."

And then the clerk drew back a step, and stood watching, while the millionaire Mr. Brown, his face burning red, and his heart beating so hard that his hand shook, set to work to forge the signature of Mr. J. P. Parkins.

Paul had taken the pen in his hand. He held it suspended over the paper. He was just about to bring it down to make the first down-stroke of the letter P, when he remembered that

he had to make the upstroke of the letter J.
For one moment of agony it seemed to him as
if he could more readily lift a ton than push the
point of his pen over that little quarter-of-an-inch
of paper. But somehow
he did it, and there was
the signature of J. P.
Parkins staring him in
the face. He looked
at it curiously, some-
what as a man might
look at a corpse of
his own killing; and
he wondered idly if
it bore the slightest
resemblance to the
signature which he
had sent in with his
deposit. The harsh
voice of the bank-clerk
woke him out of his daze.

"Ever drawn on this deposit before?" he
asked.

"No," said Paul. He did not know why,
but his heart sank within him.

The bank-clerk pushed the check back to
him across the counter, and turned sharply away
from him.

"You'll have to be identified," he said.

"But," said Paul, "I don't know anybody in
this town."

The bank-clerk merely repeated his last
words, curtly and wearily:

"You'll have to be identified."

But, at this old familiar injustice, Paul's

courage began to come back to him. He explained that he had made the deposit for the very purpose of having a sum of money at his disposal in a strange place. That this had been fully understood when the deposit was received. That it was utterly impossible for him to find anybody to vouch for his identity in a town which he had never seen before in his life. That he was willing to answer any questions that might serve to identify him, and that his signature was there for comparison with the one held by the bank.

"We don't do business in that way," said the bank-clerk. But he looked at the signature, and then hunted up Paul's account in two or three big books, and found Paul's autograph on a file, and compared the two with a quick and experienced glance. It was an awful moment for Paul, but the comparison was apparently satisfactory, for the bank-clerk showed some symptoms of relenting, or, at least, of being willing to consider the matter.

"It 's entirely irregular," he said. "What business are you traveling in? — sewing machines? — "

"No," said Paul; "I 'm not engaged in active business at present."

He was going on to say that he was traveling for his health, but it occurred to him that he did not look like a man who was traveling for his health; and he was wondering what business he could find for himself, when the clerk helped him out. "Buying real estate?" he inquired.

"I — I may look at some," answered Paul, hastily.

The bank-clerk went to the safe, and returned with the money, which he counted out very slowly in front of Paul. It was mostly in small bills. Paul took it, and was putting it in his pocket, when he was startled by the sound of a voice speaking hastily and excitedly, but in a low tone, on the other side of the door marked " Private Office." Paul felt himself growing cold.

" What 's that?" he asked, before he had time to think.

The bank-clerk had climbed back on his high stool. He did not reply to Paul's question, but he did turn his head to cast one chilly glance toward him as he said:

" You 'll probably find prices pretty stiff."

*   *   *   *   *

Paul walked toward the Ontowasco House, nursing the tail end of the bluest funk he had ever known in his life; and wondering whether he was safely through it. He did not know what happened in the bank before he had been out of it thirty seconds.

A short, fat man, with a bald head and flowing black side-whiskers, rushed furiously out of the door marked " Private Office," ran behind the

counter, and, laying violent hands upon the bank-
clerk, dragged him off his high stool and shook
him as few door-mats ever get shaken. All the
while he sputtered forth oaths and imprecations;
and the most kindly thing he said of the bank-
clerk was that he was a dod-gasted dunder-headed
fool jackass. The fat man literally foamed at
the mouth as he shook his fist in the direction
which Paul had taken.

"He 'll never come back!" yelled the fat
man. "That man will never come back, you
feather-brained mule, do you hear that? You
pudding-headed shoat, you 've lost the only new
customer we 've had in two years, with your
blamed infernal freshness. Oh, *what was* you
let into this world for?"

"Why, you told me to do it!" gasped the
bank-clerk, when he had time to speak. "Did
n't you tell me to stand him off, and give him the
impression we were doing a high-toned business
and had folks like him dropping in every day?
Did n't you tell me to meet him with dignity?"

"Meet him with dig-grandmother!" shouted
the fat man. "I did n't tell you to jump on his
neck, did I? I did n't tell you to insult him and
treat him like a sack of meal, did I? I did n't
tell you to make a confounded wild ass of the
prairie of yourself, did I? And now he 's gone,
and we 've lost him! Dignity! Dignity! Get
out of this, you gibbering loon, and go home!
You may be fit to saw wood, but you ain't fit
for one other blasted thing on this green earth.
Git!"

CHAPTER XVIII

B Y the time Paul got back to the Ontowasco House he had sufficiently emerged from his blue funk to begin to look around him with an interested eye.

He found himself in the typical old town of the middle states. Greenhill Plains was eminently respectable, of a decent antiquity, conservatively lazy, well-to-do in a comfortable, provincial way, extremely aristocratic in exactly the same way, mildly pretty, thoroughly homelike, and perfectly, wholly, completely, unshakably satisfied with itself.

Greenhill Plains had one long, wide business street with four parallel lines of trees running its whole length. All around this were modester streets, and these were again circled by the residences of the rich and great of Greenhill Plains, who dwelt in spacious squat houses of brick and stone, half citified and half countrified, each standing in the very centre of its ample grounds. In every place was a greenhouse, and the pattern of the greenhouse was an index of the owner's social character. The old conservative people of the town had greenhouses with brick foundations and sloping glass roofs. Those who belonged to the more progressive set, the leaders of advanced

thought, and the members of the Browning Club, had iron-frame houses with curved roofs. But all this Paul found out later.

At present he was content to interest himself in the Ontowasco House. He had walked in there with his wife, in time for a late breakfast, and the appearance of two dusty strangers carrying hand-bags had attracted no particular attention; for Greenhill Plains was the terminus not only of two semi-paralyzed railroads, but of three stage-routes so old that they had forgotten how to die, and of one line of horse-cars. Many country people "came up" to Greenhill Plains. They found it more convenient than New York, being much nearer, and in all other respects just as satisfactory.

The Ontowasco House was the regular first-class hotel which you will find in every town like Greenhill Plains. It was a long, three-story brown-stone building, standing on the main street, under a row of great elms. On the first floor were the hotel-office, the barroom, the barber-shop, the drug-store and the sewing-machine

agency, which was also a real-estate office. On
the broad brick sidewalk in front, the respectable
loafers of the town sat all day long, tilted back
in Shaker chairs, telling each other who was
going to be the next President of the United
States. From time to time the barroom sucked
them in through its swinging doors, and then
ejected them — as you may have seen a jelly-fish
idly winnowing his interior with little gargles of
salt water.

Paul went in at the ladies' entrance, and
climbed a steep and narrow stair, with slippery
brass plates on the steps. From the hall above,
he turned into the ladies' parlor, guided by a
smell of dried Seneca-grass, horse-hair furniture
and American-Brussels carpet. Adèle had agreed
to wait for him there because their room was very
close and small and stuffy, and looked out only
on a court above the hotel kitchen.

"I 'm afraid you 've had a stupid time waiting, my dear," he said as he entered.

"Why, not in the least, Paul," she replied,
cheerfully. "I 've had a lovely time! Oh, Paul,
do you think we could stay here a few days?
I 've enjoyed myself so much watching the
people, that I want to know what it feels like
to live here a little while. Have you ever been
in a place like this before, Paul?"

No, Paul had not. Neither of them had
ever known the deeply human joy of putting up
at a second or third class hotel and getting some
life for your money. On their wedding-trip they
had gone to the best hotels, and had been properly bored.

"You don't know how much I know al-

ready, Paul, from just sitting here in this corner
by the window. There! do you see that old
gentleman down there with his chair tilted back
against the barber-shop sign? I mean the one
with a bald head and the red
handkerchief and the funny little whiskers under his chin.
Paul, that man has had
seven drinks since you
have been away!
And do you see the
little thin old man
in the long coat?
Well, he says that
some railroad, the
something Pacific rail-
road, is going to run a
branch to Greenhill Plains;
and then it's going to be the
greatest distributing centre of the state; and that
Syracuse and those places won't be *anything* in
comparison. He says if he had a hundred thousand dollars he'd invest it all in real estate here,
this minute. But I should think if a man like
that had a hundred thousand dollars, it ought to
satisfy him, shouldn't you, Paul?"

"Why, yes," said Paul, looking down at the
group on the sidewalk. "That and a new neck-
tie. A clean collar wouldn't hurt him much,
either."

"And then, Paul," went on Adèle, "I saw a
hotel-call, and it was very interesting. A lady
came in and sent up her card to another lady
who staid in the hotel, and pretty soon the other
lady came down. They were *such* queer people,

Paul. They were n't old and they were n't young, and they wore their hair in the funniest little spit-curls you ever saw, and their clothes were *so* queer. They were expensive, you know, and I don't mean to say that they were loud or vulgar; but they had a sort of upholstery look about them."

"I know," said Paul. " 'This elegant parlor suit, $19.49.' "

"That 's just it," said Adèle. "And the ladies sat there, talking so that I could n't help hearing every word they said. It was just like rehearsing a play or something. And I found out that they both lived together in some place that they both thought a great deal of, and one of them had married a Greenhill Plains man and had come on here to live; and, as he traveled a great deal, they did n't think it worth while to keep house, and so they had come to the hotel to live. And the other lady was visiting somewhere near here, I could n't make out where, but she still lived at this place they were so fond of, and they kept talking about how the first one must miss this place she used to live in, and how delightful the society was there, and how it kept up just as it used to, and how they 'd had a perfectly lovely time last Winter, only that, of course, it was getting a little more exclusive every year. And after a while I found out what the place was — and Paul, it was She-boygan — in Wisconsin. I did n't know that there was a real Sheboygan, did you? I thought it was only a name that the funny papers had made up."

"Well," said Paul, "do you want to stay

here and make the acquaintance of Mrs. She-boygan?"

"Not exactly that," said Adèle; "but I thought we might stay here a few days just — just to take breath."

Paul thought so, too, if they could secure more comfortable quarters. And he went off to negotiate with the hotel-keeper. The hotel-keeper was rather doubtful as to whether he could find any better rooms, until Paul, who was learning something every day, asked for a large envelope, sealed up the greater part of his $250, and ostentatiously deposited it in the hotel-safe.

Five minutes later, Mr. and Mrs. Brown had the bridal apartment, consisting of three front rooms and a bathroom, on the main floor of the hotel.

"And if you *should* want to show samples," said the hotel-keeper, "we won't charge you nothing for an elegant room right across the hall, with three of the nicest tables you ever set your eyes on."

Chapter XIX

DINNER was served at one o'clock at the Ontowasco House, and it was just a section of that great dinner which is served at one o'clock on week days, and two on Sundays, in one hundred thousand hotels like the Ontowasco House, from Maine to Mendocino, and from the Mouth of the Mississippi to the Margin of Manitoba.

One day it begins with fish, and the next with soup. The soup is called barley soup or beef soup, according as the barley or beef gets the upper hand. If there are bones in the soup, it is ox-tail soup or chicken soup, according to the headwaiter's diagnosis of the bones.

Then comes roast beef, corned beef or mutton-hash, which is pronounced as if it were spelled "mutnash." Vegetables accompany this course — succotash, mashed potato with turnip, canned corn and canned tomatos — pale vegetables that died too young, because they took no interest in life; all laid out around each plate in little white china bath-tubs, and all having much the same warm, damp taste.

Then came two kinds of pie or one kind of pudding, and the bill-of-fare said "nuts and raisins." They were there, too, in the tall lattice-

work china dish in the middle of the table, and
they had been there ever since last Winter.

Now, perhaps, you are pitying the Runaway
Browns for running into such a bill-of-fare as this.
If you are, you waste the pity which you probably need for your neighbors. Let me tell you,
that with youth and appetite and an earnest
desire to have a good time it is possible to eat
that dinner, enjoy it, and thrive on it. But,
none the less, it is well to be careful about getting bits of tin-can solder between your teeth.

The Browns looked for Mrs. Sheboygan, as
they had already named her, at the dinner-table,
but she was not there. Except for the people of

the hotel and a few hurried drummers, they had
the great, low dining-room all to themselves.
It was evidently the slack season at the Ontowasco House.

After dinner, Adèle wanted to "go somewhere," and Paul went to inquire of the proprietor
where that somewhere might be.

"Well," said the proprietor, musingly, "you
've been to Greenhill Park —"

"Why, no; I have n't," said Paul.

"Oh," said the proprietor, looking at him as though he had said he had never been to church; "you 'd better go."

"And how do I go?" inquired Paul.

"Well," said the proprietor, in an injured tone, "you can walk, I suppose, if you choose, but *most* people take the horse-cars."

The proprietor turned sadly and sternly away, and Paul went out to search for the horse-cars. He found them, or, rather, it, for he encountered no other horse-car in Greenhill Plains, waiting in the street by the side of the hotel. The driver, an affable, red-faced person, said he would start in five minutes; so Paul hurried up Adèle, and they set off, with a deal of jingling, for Greenhill Park. There was no conductor, but the driver very kindly showed them how to put their fare in the box; and after they had gone a few blocks, he courteously invited them to come out and sit with him on the front platform, where he kept two camp-stools for the accommodation of his friends.

As they drove along, he enlightened them as to the personal, social, financial and commercial history and topography of the town of Greenhill Plains.

"The man who owns that house there," he said, "is what I call a gentleman. He keeps his business in Serracuse, and just lives here; and he 's worth $450,000. The man next him is worth half a million; the man next *him* ain't worth more than $50,000 or $60,000, but he 's a professor and principal of the seminary, and I suppose he 's an awful learned man. Don't seem to me, though, that if I had brains like him, I 'd

waste them on Latin and Greek, and have the
only house in the street without a cupalow."

Paul remarked upon the fact that he and his
wife were the only passengers.

"Why, yes," said the driver, cheerfully. " I
seen you was strangers in town just as soon as I
set eyes on yer. This ain't the time for the real
fashionable folks. You won't find nobody at the
Park but nurses and children. But you wait an
hour, and you 'll see more elegant people there
than you ever saw in your life before. They
come out there and tilt at them rings every afternoon, just like a tournament of ancient times.
Oh, it 's grand there, along about half-past three
or so!"

When they came in sight of Greenhill Park,
Adèle gave a little cry, half of delight and half of
disappointment. The delight was at Greenhill,
and the disappointment was at the Park. The

Browns had made their entrance into the town by the way of the valley road from the south, and they had been somewhat puzzled by the name of the place. But now, as they came out from among the trees and houses, going northward, they saw at once the reason of the name.

"You might say the rhyme and the reason, too, Paul, for it is simply *poetical!*"

Right before them stretched out a broad green plain, miles of level pasture land with hardly a tree to break the smooth expanse of green — or, rather, of greens.

"Paul, I never knew how many colors green was until now," said Adèle; "there's almost everything there from blue to yellow."

"Them's the market-gardens," explained the driver.

They did n't pay any attention to him.

That was the Plain. And beyond the Plain was the Green Hill — a beautiful, great, satisfying green hill, such as you rarely see, except on Sunday-school merit-cards; towering up, a sort of big spur from a chain of smaller hills that faded away from it on each side, modestly receding into the background.

It was certainly a delightful view, and it gave some reason for the self-complacency with which Greenhill Plains regarded itself. Not that a provincial town needs any reason for self-complacency; it always has the self-complacency, with or without reason, else it would not be a provincial town. But Greenhill Park ·was distinctly a disappointment. It was a spacious enclosure within a high board fence, whitewashed, except for a dozen painted

panels. On one of these a sign directed the
stranger to go to the Greenhill Pants Company
for pants. The other eleven panels bore the
statement, over a date of the year before
last, that applications for space in this valuable
advertising privilege should be promptly made
to P. W. Skee, Greenhill Park. An arching
sign over the entrance of the Park told that Mr.
Skee was its proprietor.

"That 's Pete Skee's house there at the
gate," said the driver; "and that 's Mrs. Skee
sitting on the piazza with the other lady. You
get your tickets of her."

When she saw them coming, Mrs. Skee
descended from the verandah of her house. Her
residence was small but ornate, like a gothic
dog-kennel. Her companion remained seated
with her hands in her lap. She wore an expression of not having noticed that the conversation had been interrupted. Mrs. Skee sold
them two tickets for fifteen cents each, and the
Browns passed in. As they went by the
verandah, Paul noticed that Adèle's eyes were
earnestly fixed upon Mrs. Skee's friend, who
was just remarking to Mrs. Skee in a tone of
stately compliment:

"How elegantly you do take to public
life, Almeena!"

Adèle touched Paul's arm. "That 's her
— she, I mean."

"Who?" asked Paul.

"The lady from Sheboygan!"

The Browns found Greenhill Park interesting, not so much for what there was in
Greenhill Park, but because they were quite

willing to find anything interesting. As the
driver had told them, the only visitors beside
themselves were, so far, a few nurse-maids and
their charges, and nothing was going on, except
a large merry-go-round worked by steam, which
was slowly revolving, bearing one solitary pas-
senger, a yellow-haired child on a giraffe. From
time to time the child wailed dismally, where-
upon his nurse broke off her conversation with
the other nurses long enough to transfer him
to an elephant or a sheep, on the back of which
he was trundled around until he wailed again,
when he was put back on the giraffe.

The Browns wandered contentedly around
and examined the various attractions of the Park.
There were a stand and seats for camp-meetings
and political gatherings. There was a sort of
race-track. There were stalls to hold cattle at
the time of the county fair. There was an ex-
hibition hall which might have held the merry-

go-round when it was stored away for the Winter. There was a base-ball ground. There were two wooden swings or scups. Then there were horse-sheds. And everywhere there was whitewash.

By-and-by a young man came in at the gate. He wore very fashionable clothes, including a light overcoat too short for him, a collar too tall for him, a fawn-colored derby hat too small for him, and a pair of yellow "spats" too conspicuous for him or for anything less notice-able than a lighthouse.

"That's one of the aristocrats," said Paul; "it's half-past-three o'clock, and the others will be along soon, I guess. Let's get up here and take in the tournament."

They climbed up on what did duty for a grand stand at the finish of the sort of race-track, and sat down to await the coming of the proud world of Greenhill Plains.

CHAPTER XX

"THEY really are coming, Paul," said Adèle, her eyes lighting up with a pleased expression. And they certainly were coming, any number of them. Within fifteen minutes the waste places of Mr. Skee's park were transformed into veritable garden spots, blooming with the flower of Greenhill Plains society. Some came on foot, but more came in carriages — carriages which were perhaps a little old-fashioned, but stately and respectable — drawn by very good horses — only they were all roadsters; not steppers. From the elevated seats which Paul and Adèle had taken, they could see the long procession strung out upon the straight highway, leading out from the town to the park, and it was a cheerful and engaging sight.

The aristocrats of Greenhill Plains seemed to be a pleasant lot of people, and to know each other very well. The men ran a little too much to spats and elegance, and the ladies all looked as though they took their fashion magazines a trifle too hard. But what do such things matter where everybody is perfectly and entirely satisfied?

Greenhill Plains's society moved around

among itself with an air of considerable distinction. Nearly every one carried his or her head a little to one side, and smiled with both corners of the mouth down. In a lower plane of usefulness the twinkling of the spats kept up the pleasant impression created by the animated faces and the New York hats.

The Browns noticed with surprise that although a great number of people had already gathered in the Park, they all kept together in that portion of the grounds nearest the gate; and not one of them so much as looked toward the race-track, across whose desolate expanse the two strangers gazed wonderingly at the interesting scene.

"Why do you suppose they don't have the tournament, Paul?" said Adèle. "Do you suppose they don't want to have it before us, and are waiting for us to go away?"

"I should think not, my dear," said Paul. "There goes a gong, now. Perhaps that will start something."

Sure enough, the sudden clang of a gong seemed to send a sharp agitation through the crowd of fashionables. It grew dense for a moment, then it opened out, and finally ten or twelve young men stepped forward into a bare space in front of the merry-go-round, and there removed their covert-coats, which they handed with dignity to other young men who took the coats over their arms and retired respectfully into the throng. Then a man in his shirt sleeves appeared, who looked, somehow, as if he must be Mr. Skee, accompanied by a negro bearing an armful of short wooden spears, each with a gilded

point. These spears he distributed among the young men, who then, apparently quite unconscious of the admiring gaze of a hundred bright feminine eyes, advanced proudly upon the merry-go-round.

"Oh, Paul," whispered Adèle, hysterically, quivering from head to foot as she touched his arm, "don't tell me that they 're really going to — Oh, Paul, is that the tournament? — It 's too absurd! I shall shriek, I know I shall!"

"Sh-h-h-h-h-h!" whispered Paul; "behave yourself."

Each of the young men mounted one of the animals of the merry-go-round; those on the elephant and other dark-colored mounts making a particularly effective display of their spats. The negro connected the steam-engine with a small orchestrion, and the machine started up, this time with an accompaniment of lively music; and, as the riders were whirled around, they endeavored, with varying degrees of skill, to catch upon their spear-points the brass curtain-rings which Mr. Skee, standing upon a three-legged stool, hung upon a lofty peg as often as was necessary.

"I 'm betting on the pearl derby, the one on the dromedary," whispered Paul.

But Adèle's eyes were running over with happy tears.

Paul would have lost his bet. The winner of the tournament was a gentleman in a white high hat, who bestrode the moolley cow. He descended from his charger amid the acclamations of his fellow-contestants and the entire gathering; and a beautiful young lady, with the prettiest possible blush on her cheeks, stepped out from the crowd and fastened a bow of red satin ribbon upon his breast with a gold baby-pin.

"My dear," said Paul, "you do wrong to laugh. This is one way of being happy; and it is far, far better than bull-fighting."

CHAPTER XXI

T was but a little past four o'clock when Paul and Adèle slipped un-noticed from the scene of mer-riment in the Park, and found themselves alone with the market-gardens and the green hill. Far down the road Greenhill Plains' one horse-car jingled merrily on its way back to the town, and they saw that they would have to wait at least an hour before it would come back to pick them up. So they decided to stroll on and examine the merit-card eminence at close quarters.

The road took them to the hill as straight as a string, but it was a long walk and a hot one. The market-gardens looked cool in their varying shades of green, but the sun has to be very low indeed, as Paul remarked, before beet-tops and lettuce-heads and tomato - vines cast a grateful shade. When they got to the hill they were quite warm, and so they set out to climb to the top to see if they could catch a breeze there. They found the breeze half-way up, and then, as they gazed down upon the market-gardens on the plain, that variegated expanse looked cool again.

But they knew well that the walk back would not be cool; and, as they reached the summit,

the thought of the
long, hot high-road far
below them made them
burst out in the simultaneous
expression of two widely differing
but equally natural wishes.

"I wish," cried Adèle, "that we did n't have
to go back at all, but could just stay here and
live."

"I wish I had a drink," said Paul.

The sound of a human snore fell upon their
ears. They looked up and saw that both their
wishes might be readily granted, for right in front
of them was a large, weather-beaten sign:

GREENHILL SUMMIT HOUSE.

The sign was the largest thing about the
house, which was perhaps as small a structure as
ever did duty for a hostelry. It looked like a mis-
calculation for a bird-house — "just as though,"
Adèle suggested, "some liberal-minded carpenter
had been told to built a home for a family of
pelicans, and, never having seen a pelican, had
misconceived the creature's size, and guessed
roughly at something half-way between an eagle
and a dodo."

A sound of snoring came from the Summit

House, although there seemed to be nobody inside. They looked in through the open door and saw a barroom not much larger than a butler's pantry. Back of this was a still smaller room with a bunk in the wall. The third room of the house was as big as the other two put together, and served as a kitchen and dining-room. All three were empty, and yet the snoring went on, heavy and regular, except when it was broken by an occasional, thick, asthmatic wheeze.

"Hi, there!" shouted Paul; "any one around?" But no answer came to him save the steady snore.

"It's almost uncanny," said his wife. "It's as though some one had left the ghost of a snore here."

"That's no ghost of a snore," said Paul; "that snore's alive, and I'll bet you a dollar it weighs two hundred pounds at the least. What's more, I'm going to find it."

He entered the house and carefully examined every room. Then he went around the house; and presently he called to Adèle from behind the kitchen chimney. Adèle hastened around and found him gazing at a very fat man with enormous clean-shaven dewlaps hanging down like wattles from the gloomiest face that ever was put on a fat man. He was fast asleep, in his shirt sleeves, his wooden chair tilted back in the angle of the projecting chimney. In front of him was an untidy ash-heap picked out with tin cans and broken crockery. Beyond this were the tangled, scrubby woods of the hilltop. His back was against the house, and the house stood between him and the broad prospect of Greenhill's check-

ered plain, and the pretty town nestling in its far-
off woods. It was a strange place to choose for
a nap, the more so that the evening sun shone
right in the fat man's face and brought the per-

spiration out in a sort of shining veil, all over his
huge features.

"Wake up!" Paul called; but he might as
well have called out to the chimney or the house.
He had to shake the fat man violently before he
could even get him to open his eyes, and then he
only stared sleepily at his visitors, and said:

"What do you want?"

"We want something to drink," said Paul.

"Water, I suppose," said the fat man, in a
dismal, despairing sort of way.

"No," said Paul; "lemonade, beer, ginger-
ale, anything."

"Only two of you?" said the fat man.

"Only two."

"What's two drinks?" the fat man demanded, as though he were deeply impressed with the hollowness of life.

"Two drinks," Paul replied with decision, "is two drinks."

"That's so," assented the fat man, more cheerily, as he left his seat; "you ain't nobody's fool, be ye?"

He mopped his face with his shirt sleeve, and led the way around the house.

"Do you generally select that spot to take your afternoon nap?" Paul politely inquired.

The fat man said "Yes."

"I should n't think it was a very good place for custom," suggested Paul.

"'T ain't," said the fat man; "ain't no custom."

"And then," remarked Adèle, dreamily, "you don't get the view; but I don't suppose you want the view when you 're asleep?"

They were just coming around the corner of the house. The fat man stopped short, and shook his fat fist at the entire landscape spread out before him.

"I don't want that view," he cried savagely, "when I 'm asleep nor when I 'm awake; when I 'm drunk, nor when I 'm sober; nor no other time. Nor you would n't," he added, impressively, "if you was in my place."

"Why, what's the matter with it?" asked Paul.

"Matter!" said the fat man, with great solemnity. "Why, look there!"

He pointed with a gesture of tragic dignity to Mr. Skee's far distant Park, from which the tide of fashion was just beginning to set back toward the town. Between one and two hundred of Greenhill's fairest and bravest were stirring up a cloud of dust that shone like gold in the late sunlight.

"There!" said the fat man; "how would you like to set here day after day and watch that, and not have one of them monkeys ever set his foot on this here hill? No, nor nobody else," he continued bitterly; "exceptin' you two, and you don't look like real drinkin' folks. I ain't had a customer this week · and last week I did n't have

nobody, only a total abstinence sewing-machine agent, who came here, by thunder, and give me a track headed 'Why Spoil Good Water?' Derned if he wer'n't crusadin' against root beer!"

The fat man brought his one table and his two chairs out from the kitchen, and his guests sat

down by the front door and ordered lemonade
and lager beer. It was evident that the resources
of the house were not calculated to meet any
great rush of custom. It took the fat man ten
minutes of arduous search to find three shriveled
and fly-specked lemons, which he assassinated
with a clasp-knife for Adèle's lemonade; then he
took his spade and began to dig in the earth in
front of the house.

"Can't I have any beer?" asked Paul.

"You can," said the fat man, reassuringly,
"just as soon as I dig it up. I can't afford to
have no ice up here this weather, and I have to
keep my beer cool the best way I can."

And after a few minutes of industrious dig-
ging, he disinterred a bottle of lager and gave it
to Paul.

The fat man brightened up and became
quite cheerful as he saw his guests enjoying their
beverages, and when Paul purchased two very
dry cigars from him, and presented him with one,
he came to the conclusion that life was worth
living, after all; and turned suddenly talkative.

He told them all about himself and his
affairs; and it seemed to afford him so much
pleasure to do so that they had not the heart to
stop him. His position was a peculiar one. The
hill and the hotel belonged to a stock-company
that was some day going to erect a great hotel
on the hilltop, and run a switchback railroad to
the summit. As yet, however, they had got no
further than to procure several valuable franchises,
and it was to keep these alive that they had engaged the fat man to conduct the Summit House,
paying him both salary and commission, so that he

could neither evade the responsibility nor yet be his own master.

"If I hang on and they hang on," said the fat man, grimly, "we 're both of us winners some day, sure; but whether we can hang on or not depends on how long we can buck against that place of Skee's down there. The company, they say it 's pretty hard work paying my salary under these circumstances, but I tell 'em that payin' my salary ain't nothin' to the moral strain of settin' here day after day and seein' that man Skee gatherin' in his ill-gotten wealth while I 'm wearin' my shirt-sleeves to save my coat."

They agreed with the fat man, whose name was Jepp, that his lot was certainly a hard one, and their assurances seemed to comfort him greatly.

"You 're right," he said; "I knowed you 'd say so. I seen discrimination in your face the

minit I set eyes on you. Where might you be
from, now?"

And to their surprise they found that Mr.
Jepp seemed to take quite as much interest in
them as he did in himself. He was not unduly
inquisitive. He seemed to care more for their
opinions, tastes and views in general; as though
he were grateful for a treat in the way of intel-
lectual companionship. They both found his conversation so soothing and agreeable that they
hardly noticed how late it was getting, until the
factory-whistles began to blow in Greenhill Plains.
Then Paul said he was afraid they must start, or
they would be late for supper at the Ontowasco
House.

"Supper!" said the fat man, in astonishment.
"My! you ain't figgerin' to get back to the Ontowasco House in time for supper, are you? How
'll you do that?"

"Why," said Paul, "we thought we'd walk
down and get the horse-car."

"The horse-car don't run no more after Mr.
Skee's Park closes. Ain't been runnin' this hour."

"Dear me!" cried Adèle. "Oh, Paul, I
can't walk all that way!"

"No, surely you can't" assented the man.
"It's better than three miles from the foot of
the hill."

"Can't we get a carriage?" inquired Paul.

"Carriage?" repeated the fat man, scorn-
fully. "Why, my dear man alive, there ain't no
carriage this side of Greenhill Plains! I'll tell
you what, though —"

But he did not tell them what. He fell
into a profound meditation, with his chin on his

hand, raising his eyes occasionally to look from Paul to Adèle.   Adèle had done her best to be a brave little girl so far; but sometimes small things are trying out of all proportion to their size, and the little woman who had uncomplainingly borne a night in a river flood felt her lip beginning to quiver as she thought of the long walk over that dusty road, in the silent, lonesome, yearning, hungry twilight.   Her eyes also began to get big, and to wink a little, but all she said as she stood and waited was:

"Oh, Paul!"

Paul hastened the current of Mr. Jepp's reflections.

"Look here," he said; "I have *got* to have a carriage or some sort of vehicle.   You fix it for me, and I 'll make it all right with you."

This is the American's password, his magic formula, in which he puts his whole faith and trust.   There are hundreds of thousands of Americans at this very moment who are laying out to get into Paradise on that phrase.

Its effect upon St. Peter remains to be seen, but it was amply sufficient for Mr. Jepp.   He pointed out that by the terms of his contract, and the franchises owned by the company, he was legally bound to keep the Summit House open every minute of the twenty-four hours; and that in consenting to go where his partners might see him, even though he left a substitute in his place, he incurred a risk of serious monetary loss. But when Paul showed a willingness to meet this danger half-way, Mr. Jepp said frankly that he could not forbear to act as one gentleman should to another, and he would walk to Greenhill Plains himself, and send a carriage out within an hour and a half — the Browns agreeing to keep the Summit House technically in full swing during his absence.

This cost Paul very nearly all the money that he had in his pocket, for the most of his two-hundred-and-fifty dollars was in the hotel safe. But then it would have been simply absurd to put a money value on the look which came into Adèle's face when she found that she did not have to walk back.

Mr. Jepp got into his coat, which was hanging in his bed-room, with remarkable agility for one so stout, and hastily gave Paul directions for the conduct of the establishment during his absence.

"There won't nobody come," he said, "except the boy with the milk; but in case anybody should, I might as well show you through the cemetery."

"The cemetery?" repeated Paul.

"Why, yes," said Mr. Jepp; "where the stuff 's buried. See? Ginger ale," he continued, pointing to the ground with his foot, "lager, sasspreller, lemon sody, root-beer; but there ain't no use diggin' for the root-beer, 'cause we 're out of it."

Here Mr. Jepp paused and looked doubtfully at Paul. "And if you, personally," he said; "I ain't speaking for the general public, should want a little drop of anything more reachin' than slops, why I 'll show you where to get it." And, leading Paul behind the bar, he discovered to him a small cupboard in whose depths lurked several uninviting bottles, each of which con-

tained what might be called sample dregs of
ardent spirits.

"There!" said Mr. Jepp, with so much
pride that Paul could only thank and pity him.

"Make yourself free of everything," was
Mr. Jepp's parting injunction; "the house is
yours, and if your lady wants to lay down on my
bed she 'll find it clean and comfortable. If
there 's anything in the house you want to eat,
why, it 's yours. Make yourself right to home.
But I 'll be back inside of one hour and a half.
Call it," he concluded, with an air of cautious

speculation, "one hour and twenty minutes — me
and the carriage."

He started down his winding way, and once

more the Browns were left alone; and the cool shades of the evening began to settle down upon the sylvan gloom around them.

Adèle slipped her hand into Paul's. From far below them Mr. Jepp's voice rose with a cheerful ring.

"One hour," it said, "*and* twenty minutes."

CHAPTER XXII

FOR a while it was pleasant sitting up there with all the world at their feet. There is always something agreeable about being on a mountain-top and feeling exalted above the rest of humanity. That is why we figure heaven as a place high up in the air, and why Bostonians live on Beacon Hill. Broken murmurs of the busy life below them came up, as they lay on the short, wiry grass under the gnarled trees, and watched the setting sun. Cows mooed afar off, and their bells tinkled faintly. The thrushes were singing their evening song, which, with some thrushes at least, is quite different from their matinée performance, and particularly appropriate to the season; which has led me to believe that the thrush is rather a superior bird in his way.

But after a while it grew monotonous, and they began to speculate as to when the boy would arrive with the milk. They had watched Mr. Jepp out of sight. They had explored every nook and corner of the Summit House, and now there was nothing between them and utter mental stagnation but the coming of the boy with that milk. It was a quarter of eight, and Mr. Jepp had been gone an hour and forty-five minutes when the boy appeared. He was a common-place boy

with a freckled face, who did not look as surprised at seeing them as they somehow thought
he ought to look.

"Where's *he*?" the boy inquired carelessly.

"Do you mean Mr. Jepp?" asked Paul.

"Yep," said the boy.

"Mr. Jepp," said Paul, "has gone to Greenhill Plains; he will be back shortly."

"No he won't," said the boy.

"What do you mean?" demanded Paul.

"Did he leave you here to take care of
things till he came back?" the boy asked, in a
decisive tone.

"Yes," replied Paul, rather faintly.

"Then he won't come back till he's had his
drunk out," said the boy. "He never does when
he can get 'em to stay. Did he get any money
out of you?"

"Some — " stammered Paul; "that is — well
— four dollars — "

The boy whistled.

"That will keep him going 'most a week,"
he said, as he slung his empty milk-pail over
his arm.

"But here, hold on!" cried Paul, for the
boy was already starting off, "there must be some
mistake about this. Are you sure? How do
you know?"

"He's my dad," said the boy, as he moved
out into the tangled hollow of the wood.

————

Paul was almost afraid to face Adèle with
this piece of news; but she took it much more

philosophically than he had any reason to expect she would.

"I 'm sure it might be a great deal worse, Paul," she said. "The bed-room *is* perfectly nice and clean, for I 've looked to see, and if we could find something for supper we should do very well. If I could get something to eat I think I could stand anything; and really, do you know, Paul, I was getting very tired of the Ontowasco House. I was just thinking about it when you were talking to the boy."

"Adèle, you are an angel," said Paul.

"Nonsense!" said Adèle, "though of course I am glad, dear, if you think so."

They investigated the larder of the Summit

House with better results than they had dared to
hope for, although these results were no more
than ham and potatos, and something that had
aspirations in the way of being coffee. The sight
of a couple of lonely, gawky hens, that looked
as if they were trying to make up their minds to
give over domesticated life altogether and adopt
the profession of wild-fowl, suggested the possibility of eggs; and search under the bushes
behind the house was rewarded with a couple in
delightfully fresh condition. And as folks who
have a ham-and-egg appetite and the ham-and-
eggs to go with it are not in the least to be
pitied, it was naturally enough two contented and
happy Browns who stretched themselves out an
hour or so later to watch the Summer moon climbing up the sky.

When a young couple can only look back
on a courtship conducted in a Philadelphia semi-
nary for young ladies, under what may be called
circumstances of aggravated bread-and-butter and
slate-pencil, mountain-tops and Midsummer moonlight nights come in uncommonly handy, even if
they are a little late. Paul lit his pipe, and they
lay out in the white glare and looked up at the
stars.

"They were very good, Paul," said Adèle,
"and I am glad you liked them; but where was
it that we had such delicious ones on our wed-
ding trip?"

"At Saratoga, dear. Don't you remember?
they were Saratoga chips."

"Oh, yes!" said Adèle; "how stupid of me
to forget it! I must learn to make those. Do
you think I could?"

"Oh, you could learn to make anything!" said Paul, with perfect confidence.

May be you don't think that was romance. Well, you don't know; you simply don't know.

It was so much romance that they both started up almost guiltily, as a strange sound suddenly reached them from far down the mountain-side.

"Why, Paul!" cried Adèle; "it must be Mr. Jepp with the carriage. What shall we do? I don't want to go back to the Ontowasco House after making up that lovely bunk."

"Well, we'll tell *him* to go back," said Paul. "He can have our room at the Ontowasco House, and we'll swop with him. Perfectly simple."

The sound of wheels slowly drew nearer as the vehicle crawled up the mountain-side. At last it came to a place where the twisting and

doubling road ran through a cleared spot, and
here the Browns, looking down, saw that it was
not a carriage, nor yet Mr. Jepp, but a ramshackle farm-wagon driven by a singularly lean
man, with a weedy, long, goat-like beard. Adèle
looked a little frightened.

"Who can it be, Paul?" she whispered.

"I don't know," replied Paul. "Some farmer
going home, I suppose. I only hope he does n't
want to stay here to-night, because — "

"Because what?" asked Adèle.

"Because he shan't."

But it looked as though their hospitality was
to be put to the test, for when the stranger
reached the summit of the hill, he hitched his
horse, which was as ramshackle as the wagon,
to a convenient tree, and slowly advanced toward
them.

"Evenin'," said he.

"Good evening," said Paul.

"Seasonable night," said the stranger. "Jepp
around?"

"Mr. Jepp," said Paul, "is in Greenhill
Plains."

"Yes," said the stranger, reflectively; "yes,
I seen him there. Fuller 'n a tick."

"May I ask," inquired Paul, "if it is cus-
tomary for Mr. Jepp to get intoxicated?"

"Oh, yes!" said the stranger; "quite so."

He still stroked his beard, while his eyes
wandered vacantly around.

"Quite so," he repeated reflectively; "quite
so."

Paul grew impatient.

"Can I do anything for you?" he said at

last. "I am in charge here during Mr. Jepp's absence. I am sorry I can't put you up, as the accommodations of the establishment are rather limited; and I can't give you any supper, for my wife and I have eaten all there was; but anything else that I can do for you—"

"I 'm going home," said the man with the beard, "and I don't want no supper." Still he stood in a doubtful, uneasy sort of way, as though he wanted something and did n't care to mention it.

"Is there anything you 'd like to drink?" inquired Paul. "There is some nice, cool ginger-ale."

The strange man pulled at his beard in an agony of indecision. At last he spoke.

"I 'll take a cocktail," he said.

"I am afraid," began Paul—but the stran-ger raised a pair of mournful eyes toward heaven.

"I could n't take nothing only a cocktail," he said. "I feel a kind of goneness here." He laid his hand upon his stomach, and Paul per-ceived that he did, indeed, look faint and pale, and appeared to be suffering.

"I hate to do it," he said sadly, as though he were speaking to himself.

Paul felt his sympathies aroused. "I 'll do what I can, sir," he said; "but I 'm afraid this is not the place to come to for a good cocktail. However, if you feel faint, I suppose the liquor will do you good, any way."

He started for the bar, but the man held out a hand as if to detain him.

"No; don't," he said; and then he checked himself as suddenly.

"Yes," he said; "go ahead, I 'll take it."

Paul went behind the bar and lit the kero-sene lamp. There he was joined by Adèle.

"Paul," said she, "that man is deceiving you. I know it."

"How do you know?" asked Paul.

"Because I saw his expression as soon as he saw you go in here. Paul, I don't believe he 's got any more stomach-ache than you or I have."

"Hush, my dear," said Paul, for the man had already followed them in, and was standing by the doorway.

"I don't care, dear," said his wife; "I 'm right; you 'll see if I 'm not. That man 's a humbug and a hypocrite. You may trust a woman's instinct. I am perfectly certain of it."

Now, there are few harder moments in a man's life than the moment when his wife tells him that another man in whom he has trusted is abusing his confidence. It is a moment that has been too much for the good sense and discretion of experienced and middle-aged men, long past hugging the delusions of their youth; and that it should move a comparatively green youngster to indiscretion is not to be wondered at. Paul looked in angry doubt at the dark figure by the door, and thought he could detect something deceitful and dishonest in the very turn of the stranger's head. He felt all the irritation of the honest man, who takes his drink and sees no harm in it, for the man who takes it in violation of his own principles. And, just as a sense of this feeling came over him, temptation in its most trying form put itself in his way. For I take it that no American is more keenly tempted than when the spirit of revenge and his sense of humor work together. Paul's eye had fallen upon a bottle labeled "benzine."

"By thunder!" he said to himself; "that fellow shall have a cocktail, and he shall not forget it in a hurry, either."

"There!" he said, pushing across the counter the drink he had mixed, and his gorge rose as he saw the stranger come forward and continue his curious pantomime of hesitancy.

"What a humbug!" thought Paul; "and all that nonsense for the benefit of two people who don't care a stiver what he drinks, or how he drinks it."

The stranger came up to the bar in a doubtful, nervous way, as though even yet he had not made up his mind, and Paul gave the drink a final, disgusted shove. This seemed to decide him. He pushed back a coin to Paul, and Paul slung it contemptuously into the till. The man grasped his glass and drained it at one draught. Then an expression of horror came over his face — an expression of horror which Paul never forgot to his dying day. The expression of horror was succeeded by one of profound doubt and wonderment. Then the man smelled of his glass, then he lifted the flap of his old-fashioned frock coat and smelled of that; and Paul knew that his sin had found him out; and that whatever that man knew about cocktails, he knew benzine when he smelled it. He stood almost paralyzed while the stranger walked solemnly around the bar, peered into the little cupboard, found the benzine bottle, examined the label, and then straightened himself up with a sigh of satisfaction. All trace of hesitancy had disappeared from the countenance of the man with the goat-like beard. He looked at Paul for one moment with an expression of withering calm.

"I did n't mean to," he said, "but I don't mind doing it now. Young man, I 'm the Sheriff of North Greenhill County, and I arrest you for selling liquor without a license."

Chapter XXIII.

THE moonlight shone brightly down upon the upper end of North Greenhill County — not the upper end of Greenhill County, which is a pleasant and civilized lowland, but of North Greenhill County, which is a lonely northward upland, spotted with abandoned farms.

With its last rays that night it looked down upon one of the most desolate of all these neglected ghosts of homesteads. It may have been a large farm at one time, but it had evidently been so many kind of farms in the course of its struggle for existence, that its unlucky acres had long ceased to give the faintest suggestion of pride

or promise, or even of plain, ordinary self-respect.
There were wrecks of stock-barns and stables;
there were stubble-fields where corn and rye had
grown; there were broad patches where stray
pumpkins and lonely watermelons were all that
was left to tell of some forgotten period of culti-
vation; there were pear and apple orchards gone
to wrack and ruin. And apparently one of the
latest phases of the farm's struggle for existence
had been a desperate attempt at poultry-raising,
for two or three home-made brooder-houses and
chicken-runs stood in the back yard of the old
frame farm-house, and showed fewer signs of
decay than the dismal homestead itself.

At the end door of the newest of these struc-
tures — a low building with a narrow-paned skylight in its sloping roof — stood three figures: a
good-looking young man and a good-looking
young woman, both quite pale in the flooding
moonlight, and a lean, long man with a goat-like
beard. This latter was speaking in a tone between dubiousness and determination.

"It may be an outrage," he said, "but it 's
all the place I 've got to put you, and it 's all the
lock-up the town 's had in three years. If your
lady don't like it, she can sit outside; she ain't
under no arrest."

"Oh, no, Paul!" cried Adèle; "I 'll go in
there with you."

"Very well, Marm," said the Sheriff; "the
last man in there was a nigger, and he was perfectly satisfied."

A minute later he had locked the door upon
his two captives. He took a step toward the
house, then he stopped and seemed to hesitate.

But, after a moment, as though to give himself
courage, he lifted the skirt of his coat to his nose;
and, as he smelled of it, a look of stern resolution
came into his face, and he proceeded with a firm
step toward the house.

Paul Brown gazed after him through the
narrow parallel bars of the skylight-frame, in
which a few panes of glass were still to be seen.

He clenched his hands, and his chest heaved.
When he saw the farm-house door close behind
the Sheriff, he slowly took off his coat, folded it,
laid it upon an inverted water-pail in the corner,
and with a courtly gesture invited his wife to take
the seat thus prepared. Then, without saying a
word, he proceeded to try the roof and the sides
of the house with his shoulder.

The gentlemen who can put their shoulders
through inch plank and two-by-three joist may be
seen almost any evening at any well-regulated
Bowery theatre, escaping from loathsome dun-

geons and burning garrets, generally with a lovely heroine thrown over the shoulder that is not doing the bucking. But then they have six nights practice a week, to say nothing of matinées; and as this was the first time that Paul Brown had tried it, it was no wonder that he failed. When he found that he could not break out, he sat down on a box by the side of his wife and hid his face in his hands. Something shook his shoulders. They were only flesh and blood, after all. When his wife saw his shoulders shake, she put both her arms around his head and said:

"I don't mind, dear."

But Paul minded, and he knew in his inmost soul that he had good reason to mind. So far, in their little journey into the world, they had met with ill-luck, discomfort, privation, and even with physical danger. They had encountered suspicion and rude treatment: they had been cheated and imposed upon. And they had taken all that had come with light and contented hearts, as their share of the bad chances in the game of life.

But now they stood face to face with the bitter opposition of personal malignity, and Paul knew that all the pleasant and joyous spirit had gone out of their wayfaring, even if he were able to save this brave little wife from cruel annoyance and humiliation, such as a mean and narrow-minded yokel might delight to inflict, in the gratification of a petty spite.

And, no matter how long out of service it may be, a chicken-house never entirely recovers from the smell.

Suddenly Paul felt his wife's encircling arms twitch violently,

"Paul," she whispered, releasing him, "look there!"

As Paul looked up, he could not check a quick, cold chill about the roots of his hair. Straight in front of him, clearly visible through the skylight, stood a gigantic coal-black negro, stock-still in the moonlight, like some uncanny monster out of the Arabian Nights. There was something frightful about the huge creature as he stood there, silent and motionless, staring at them with his broad, brute-like face. It was not until Paul observed a slight but regular lateral movement of the lower jaw, that he recognized the fact that a tie of common humanity bound him to the strange apparition. Paul smoked and the negro chewed, but tobacco belongs to the world of men and not to the world of spirits.

A gleam of hope sprang up before the prisoners, as the negro, with a sudden, cat-like movement, advanced toward them, and grinned

at them through a broken pane. It was a friendly grin; a kindly grin; a broad grin, perhaps; but it seemed to them a very beautiful grin.

"D' ye want to get out, boss?" he whispered. And the first twang of angel harps could not have sounded more sweet.

"I DO!" said Paul, with a vehemence and emphasis which he had been saving up for some time.

"What 's it wuth?" asked the negro, flashing his white teeth in the moonlight.

"Anything!" said Paul, who felt for the moment that if that negro wanted the Congo River he ought to have it.

"Anything ain't nothing, once you get out," said the negro with a cheerful laugh.

Paul saw that he had to deal with a man of the world, and went down into his pocket for his last handful of change.

He held it to the light in the hollow of his palm. The negro's face lit up with the illumination of avarice.

"Hand it out here, boss," he said.

"Hand *us* out," Paul said briefly and decisively.

Caucasian and Ethiopian gazed into each other's eyes. It was a struggle of will; and the Caucasian triumphed. The Ethiopian's eyes fell.

"I 've got to trust to your honor as a gentleman, boss," he said. "What are you in for? Horses?"

"Confound your black impudence!" began Paul; and instantly a smile of happy confidence irradiated the hitherto doubtful face of the colored stranger.

"*Knowed* you was a gentleman, boss," he said, promptly. "Now, just step to that eend over there and put yo' hand up to the roof. Feel a hook and staple thah, sah? Yas? Well, jest onhitch that hook. Now push the skylight up. Dere you are, sir. Lemme hold it open till your lady gets out."

In a dazed sort of way, Paul stepped out and helped Adèle after him, while the negro stood by, amiably grinning and holding the ventilating skylight open. In a dazed sort of way Paul paid over the remaining change in his pocket, to the last cent. In a dazed sort of way he inquired in what direction the railroad lay; and in a dazed sort of way the two Browns went toward the station.

When the midnight train roared on its southward way, after a brief stop at a little branch station just above the border-line of New York and New Jersey, it left behind it a station-agent and a flagman, who gazed speculatively, by the light of a couple of lanterns, at a curious little heap of personal belongings on the shelf in front of the ticket-seller's window.

"Mighty fishy security for two tickets to the Junction, Jim," said the station-agent, reflectively; "but I done it on *her* face, and I 'll bet I don't get left, neither."

He turned over the articles in the heap before him. They were as follows:

One nickel-plated Waterbury watch,

One lady's pencil case,

One gentleman's silk pocket-handkerchief,

One penknife with a corkscrew in it,

One small onyx scarf-pin,

One silver match-safe,

One very dry cigar,

One visiting card:

Mr. Paul Brown.

CHAPTER XXIV

T was just six o'clock of a Summer's morning. The sun was lifting a soft opal mist from off a little Jersey town which peeped out of a nest of young green trees. A couple of young people, who looked somewhat the worse for wear, turned into a broad cheerful street with taller trees along the edge of the roadway, and with a row of low, spreading-roofed cottages on each side. Every house stood in a large generous patch of lawn or garden. At the further end of the street stood an old white church with a great pillared portico in front.

The young people turned into the gateway of one of the prettiest houses on the street. The roses were blooming in the front yard. The gravel walks were as neat as a new pin. Ampelopsis climbed over half the house; and there were scarlet runners on the sunny side.

One of the couple was a young man. The other was a young woman. When they got inside the gate they looked at each other, and the young woman said to the young man:

"Paul, do you know where we are?"

The young man looked with inquiring interest at the ampelopsis and the scarlet-runners.

"Paul," said the young woman, "we are At Home."

Paul felt that some religious ceremony was needed, so he took off his hat. Then they went into the house. The bright morning light filtered through the closed blinds into a pretty little parlor. The two young people, who seemed very disheveled, indeed, once they were inside the house, stood in the middle of the room and looked about them.

"It needs pictures," said Adèle, "and flowers and books and nonsense things. And, Paul, it's going to have them!"

But Paul was not thinking about the future adornment of the room. He was a man, and he hated to be laughed at. His eyes sought his open desk. He walked straight across the room, picked up a large unopened envelope that was lying upon it, and with a look of rapture he held it up for his wife to see.

"Yes, sir; I took the liberty of not delivering it, sir," said a familiar voice.

They turned, and saw Mrs. Wimple standing in the doorway.

"Lord bless your dear souls!" said Mrs. Wimple. "I knew you would n't be no year away." She took off Adèle's hat and gave her a motherly kiss. "Now you go right upstairs," and get yourselves ready, and I 'll have breakfast on the table in no time. You look like you 've been traveling all night. I kinder s'picioned you 'd be home to-day, and so I raised some of them biscuit over night, that you say you like so dreffle much. And there 's five cucumbers on the vine in the back yard."

And she sailed off, leaving a stream of talk behind her, and went into the kitchen, where she talked right on, to the cat, in the gladness of her heart.

Mr. and Mrs. Paul Brown went upstairs, where they had an orgy with cold water, clean soap, and soft towels. Then they came downstairs, and Adèle led the way out-doors, and they walked down the neat paths among the flowers. Paul thought she was going to pluck a nosegay for the breakfast table, but she was not. She only moved among the flowers, caressing them with the tips of her fingers, patting their heads, and touching their cool cheeks as though they had been so many children. A great fat sleepy stock shook down a dash of water, and wet her hand, as she chucked him under his white double chin; but she only laughed.

"Paul," she said, "do you know how long our year has been?"

"What year?" asked Paul.

He was doing so much thinking that he was stupid for the moment.

"The year that we ran away for," said Adèle. "It began last Monday, and it ends to-day; and to-day 's Saturday."

"I knew it was n't a year," said Paul; "but there was a good deal of it while it lasted."

"Yes," assented Adèle; "and do you know what *we* 've been?"

"A pair of fools," answered Paul promptly.

"Yes, dear," said his wife, taking his face between the tips of her dewy fingers and pulling it down, so that she could look into his eyes; "but *nice* fools, don't you think?"

"Breakfast is ready," said Mrs. Wimple.

THE END.

One of the special weekly attractions of our humorous contemporary PUCK, is a short story which does n't much resemble short stories published elsewhere.

"MAVERICKS"

they have been called of late, and "Mavericks" is the title of a pretty volume just published, containing about twenty of them by as many writers. Among the contributors are W. J. Henderson, Brander Matthews, Madeline Bridges, George H. Jessop, Tudor Jenks, Flavel S. Mines, R. K. Munkittrick, and PUCK's editor, Mr. Bunner, whose "Short Sixes" formed the initial volume of the series of which "Mavericks" is the latest issue. To any one in search of something which will make him laugh this little book may be safely commended. The pictures, of which there are many, are quite as funny as the tales, and are all by PUCK's artists. —*N. Y. Herald.*

In Boards, $1.00.   In Paper, 50 Cents.

All Booksellers.

By Mail, from the Publishers, on receipt of price.

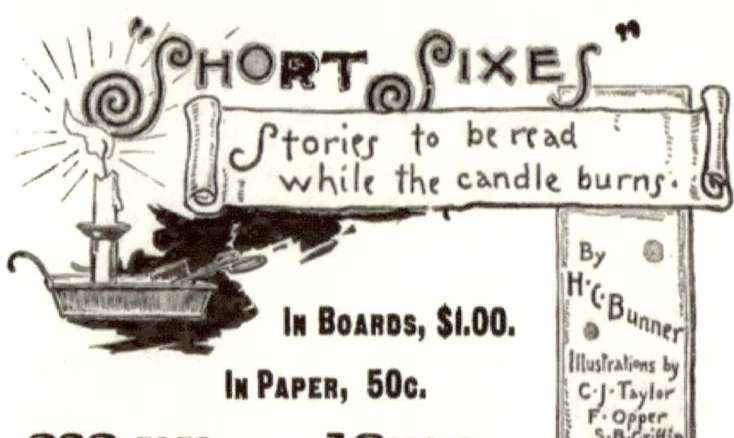

"SHORT SIXES"

Stories to be read while the candle burns.

By H. C. Bunner

Illustrations by
C. J. Taylor
F. Opper
S. B. Griffin

IN BOARDS, $1.00.

IN PAPER, 50c.

232 pp.   16mo.

Illustrated by C. JAY TAYLOR.

"THE TENOR."
"COL. BRERETON'S AUNTY."
"A ROUND-UP."
"THE LOVE-LETTERS OF SMITH."
"HECTOR."
"THE NICE PEOPLE."
"MR. COPERNICUS AND
              THE PROLETARIAT."
"A SISTERLY SCHEME."
"ZOZO."
"THE OLD, OLD STORY."
"THE TWO CHURCHES OF 'QUAWKET."
Illustrated by F. OPPER.

"ZENOBIA'S INFIDELITY."
"THE NINE CENT-GIRLS."
Illustrated by SYD B. GRIFFIN.

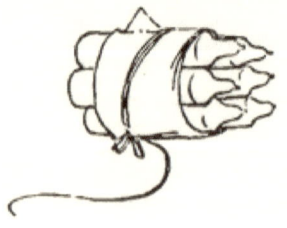

For Sale by all Booksellers and Newsdealers
Mailed on Receipt of Price by the
"PUBLISHERS OF PUCK." New York.

The beauty of James L. Ford's

HYPNOTIC TALES

is that they are intensely full of modern
New York. Those who read them simply
because they suspect that they are humorous will find to their surprise a lot of
admirable satire. It is hard to imagine a
better presentation of certain blemishes on
the police department than " The Detective's Tale." In " The Genial's Tale " he
has for the first time classified a type and
given it a name ; so that now when you
speak of a Genial, everybody knows what
you mean. Among the other sketches the
best are " The Rich Presbyterian's Tale,"
and " At the Chromo-Literary Reception "
— the latter a perfect picture of the sort of
thing that the " New York Correspondent "
of the *Bungtown Bugle* revels in. — *Life.*

In Boards, $1.00.   In Paper, 50 Cents.

All Booksellers.

By Mail, from the Publishers, on receipt of price.

Stories founded on Fiction.

By C. H. AUGUR. Illustrated by C. J. TAYLOR.

CONTENTS.

HANDSOMELY BOUND IN BOARDS, $1.00.   IN PAPER COVER, 50c.

Of all Booksellers. By mail from the publishers on receipt of price.

* * * * *   * * *   * * * * *

TO PUCK,

whose enduring confidence in the foolishness of mortals has brought about the publication of these HALF-TRUE TALES, *this volume is respectfully dedicated.*

www.ingramcontent.com/pod-product-compliance
Lightning Source LLC
Chambersburg PA
CBHW030121030726
47498CB00007B/2498